Saint John's Ambulatory

Manulque murum femper

ED CHARLTON

Also by Ed Charlton

The Problem With Uncle Teddy's Memoir

The Able Serial:

Able

Sopha

TMV

Anir

Saint John's Ambulatory

ISBN
Paperback 978-1-935751-46-5
eBook 978-1-935751-47-2

Published in the United States of America by
Scribbulations LLC
Kennett Square, Pennsylvania
U.S.A.

This book is the second of a nontraditional trilogy starting with
The Problem with Uncle Teddy's Memoir. *Reading the previous book is recommended but not required as this book, while being contemporaneous and sharing certain elements with the other, contains no Uncle Teddy.*

The action takes place in England between 2010 and 2013.
The characters are British and speak accordingly. Spelling and punctuation are (more or less) American English.

A partial and apocryphal Glossary of Unfamiliar Terms is included at the end to aid the bewildered.

Dedication

To those keeping traditions alive.

Best wishes!

E) Charlton

CHAPTER ONE

Sunday afternoon, Monday morning

The bishop sighed. "He has to go, I'm afraid, Geoff."

On his phone, the image of a priest nodded, "Okay, decision made. Which lands me with the problem of where to put him now. Do you have a replacement in mind, Dave?"

Bishop David Davidson, "The Dave" to his friends, shook his head. "Just find someone whose head is in this century."

"...And not up his own arse."

"Preferably. Shouldn't have let him get so entrenched at St. John's. My fault."

"Do I tell him, or will you go over there?"

Dave shrugged. "I'll do it. Let's get the new man sorted first."

And so, Fr. Bartholomew Samuels' professional fate was sealed; no more to shepherd the parish of St. John's In The Green, demoted, put out to grass in some remote institution from where his superiors would hear no more complaints. A fate he was only spared by unexpectedly— and unwillingly—entering into his eternal reward that same night.

* * *

The text from Fr. Geoff came as Dave was finishing breakfast.

"Police @ St Johns Samuels dead possibly murdered"

He called out from the dining room, "Sherry!"

His secretary, Sherry, came running. "Dave? You alright? What's the matter?"

"Something's happened at St. John's. Cancel today—everything."

She nodded. "Not the usual?"

"He might have been killed."

"Oh my..."

She came back after a moment with her tablet. "You're at your sister's tonight."

He nodded. "I hope I'll still do that."

She talked as she read. "I'll talk to the Life committee, two other meetings this afternoon...I'll call them. Lunch was with the chief rabbi. You shouldn't miss that."

"I know. Tell him exactly why, or he'll be offended. And tell him I would have sent him a text if he'd only get a smartphone."

Sherry smiled. "Will do."

"Tell Geoff I'm on my way there. Try and contact whoever you can at the Met. Let them know I'm coming to St. John's."

Sherry looked doubtful, "I'll do my best. Will you drive yourself?"

The bishop thought for a moment, wiping the last of breakfast from his mouth, "No, order a taxi. That way I can impose myself. Oh...God help us!"

* * *

The police tape was across the end of the road. As the taxi pulled up alongside, a woman constable waved the driver on. He wound down his window and jerked his thumb back toward his passenger. Dave emerged and checked the driver would be paid from the diocesan account, giving time for the constable to duck under the tape and step toward them.

"Road's closed! You'll have to move on!"

"Good morning, Constable," Dave began.

"Road's closed! You'll have to move on!"

"I'm an auxiliary bishop of Southwark..."

"I don't care if you're the fucking pope, mate. It's a crime scene. Move on!"

"And I'm the victim's boss and responsible for this property. You'll take me to the officer in charge and be quick about it!"

She looked him up and down. "Wait here."

She was gone for several minutes. After the taxi had left, no one else came by to stand or look.

2

The road blocked by the twisting blue-and-yellow ribbon was not long. To the left was a small park edged by an iron railing, to the right the church itself, and beyond it the rectory. Across the other end of the road, to both left and right, was a towering mass of scaffolding, incomplete yellow stone walls, and sheets of dirty white plastic billowing in the breeze. The new building, even unfinished, dwarfed the street and everything in it—namely two police cars, two unmarked cars, and a white van. The blue and red flashers were still pulsing on one car. Despite the even gray daylight, the alternating shadows of colors arched up the plastic of the building site, across the rectory, and along the church walls like a giant puppet show.

The smell of car exhaust drifted round him as he waited. He watched the stooping figures of several uniformed policemen searching the park.

The woman PC and a man in plainclothes stepped out of the rectory door. She pointed up the street toward him. The man nodded, and they walked slowly up the pavement, casting shadows on the pulsing blue and red of the church wall.

"Good morning, Fred," said The Dave.

"Morning, Dave. Can you show the constable some identification, please?"

Dave fished out his driving license from his wallet. "Is that good enough?"

She took it and read it carefully. "Sorry. Good morning, er, Reverend?"

"Please...call me Dave."

The detective smiled and said quietly to the PC, "We will afford the bishop every courtesy."

She replied stiffly, "Yes, sir!"

To Dave, Fred said, "You know the victim, right?"

"I know Fr. Samuels very well. Is it he?"

"Ah. We...we're not officially sure. Perhaps you could give us a preliminary identification. We'll need a formal ID later, but it would help if you could."

Dave nodded. "Of course. What exactly has happened?"

"Well..." They started to walk toward the rectory. "As you'll soon see, it isn't really clear. The victim is dead. No doubt there."

"God receive his soul," Dave muttered.

Fred continued, "A parishioner found the body when no one showed up to do the 6:30 service. Er...did you have your breakfast?"

"I did, why?"

The PC replied with a smile, "You might not have it for much longer."

Fred gave her a look and nodded toward the tape and the end of the street. She rolled her eyes and, smiling, turned back to take up her position again. A young man in a bright yellow cycling suit, with a bright yellow bicycle to match, was waiting for her.

"It's as gruesome a scene as I've come across, I'm afraid. I'll give you booties and gloves to put on; our scene-of-crime officers aren't quite done yet."

"Understood. Can I ask why you are on this one? You don't usually 'do' murders, do you?"

"No...," the detective sighed, "not really. But you can guess why."

Dave nodded. "Again, understood."

The rectory of St. John's In The Green was a modest old house dating from before the Second World War. The front door opened onto a vestibule and staircase. Rooms went off to the right and to the left; the kitchen occupied the rear. As Dave pulled blue hospital booties over his shoes, he watched two men in baggy plastic overalls packing instruments into cases. He stood silently in the kitchen doorway. He was old enough to remember real butcher's shops: sawdust on the floor, quartered animals on hooks, and this smell—the smell of blood.

The table and chairs were in disarray; the body stretched out in front of the sink. A lake of blood encompassed the body and spread along to the right where the priest's head had rolled. Beyond them, a door was open to the small passage linking the rectory to the back of the church. To the left of the kitchen was a small scullery with a partitioned-off toilet. It was here Dave threw up, as had one of the constables earlier.

Fr. Samuels still had the shock of white hair that, in life, had given him a wild-man-of-the-woods silhouette. His perpetual frown of disapproval, however, was lifted, in death, by a simple grin.

The detective had asked, "Can you identify the victim for me?"

When he returned from losing his breakfast, Dave nodded and said, "The Reverend Bartholomew Samuels, God have mercy on his troubled soul."

CHAPTER TWO

Monday evening

"Get a move on! Your uncle will be here in a minute!"

"I know, Mum, I know! And it's Uncle Dave. He's only a bishop—well auxiliary bishop—not the pope. It's not a state occasion."

"You haven't seen him in a year. At least show some interest!"

Peter Trowbridge put down his book and helped his mother lay the table.

"We've FaceTimed. And it's you he's coming to see too."

His mother gave him a look. "He's not after me to sign up."

Peter sighed. "He's going to be disappointed."

Helen Trowbridge laughed quietly. "Good. I still fancy myself as a grandmother."

"Patience, woman!" he joked.

She handed him the napkins. "I," she paused, "was pregnant a second time at your age."

"Is that a comment on the reticence of my generation or the unbridled passion of yours?"

"Oh, I could tell you a thing or two!" she laughed.

"I hope you won't. Especially not in front of the bishop!"

"Really, Peter, twenty-five is getting on a bit nowadays."

Peter stopped and thought. "Seems to me like I just left school. When did you work out what you wanted to be when you grew up?"

Helen thought for a moment. "Never did. You lot happened. Your father...left us. Keeping going was as much 'working out' as I've ever done."

"Well then! That's me off the hook. I'll 'keep going' for a while longer."

"That usually involves your own place, employment, let alone..."

Peter interrupted. "I only just got back, and you want rid of me already?"

"Uncle Dave is sure to ask you. If you're not going to be a priest... what else?"

The doorbell rang.

"Hello, sister-mine!" said The Dave, "And there he is! Taller and mightier than ever!"

"Hi, Uncle Dave, good day at the office?"

A chill ran through the bishop. "Ah. No, not so much..."

Helen frowned. "Whatever is the matter?"

"I'll tell you later. Don't want to spoil dinner."

At the table, Peter found he had to make a lot of the conversation.

"The retreat was good. You were right about Fr. Finnegan. Describing him as 'a bit of a character' doesn't do it at all!"

"Yep. He's out there, isn't he? But one of the best, one of the best..."

Dave stopped, lost in his thoughts; his sister and nephew exchanged a worried glance.

"Um," Peter began, "I guess I need to tell you I've decided..."

"Hmm? What about?"

"About my not being a priest..."

"Oh, yes. Probably wise..."

Helen sat up straight but said nothing.

"Really?" asked Peter.

Dave seemed to come back fully to the present. "It's a tough job...but it's more. We don't call it a vocation for nothing. If you're called, you're called. If you're not, best not to get too invested. So what decided you, hmm?"

Peter glanced at his mother and said, "The three things I told you would be a problem."

"Poverty, chastity, and obedience?"

"And not necessarily in that order."

Dave laughed for the first time that evening. "I know, I know. But let me tell you, as a diocesan priest, the poverty is only in terms of what we pay you. Come from money and you'd be okay."

Peter gave his mother a theatrical glare. "Unless she's keeping something from me, that would still count as a reason."

"And the chastity...well, there are those who make a parade of their celibacy, while letting that chastity thing go by the wayside. And as for obedience! Oh, they're like cats! When I say 'no' they understand 'not while the boss is watching'!" He was lost in thought again for a moment. "So, what will you do?"

Helen slid her chair back and quietly said, "I'll get dessert."

Peter squinted at her and said, "Well...we were just talking about that before you arrived. Mother seems keen on me moving out again."

His uncle nodded. "What are you doing at the moment? I can't remember what you're working at."

Peter shook his head. "How do you think I have time to go traveling to Nepal or to spend a week at Fr. Finnegan's retreat?"

Where Peter had expected a joke or a word of advice, instead he found his uncle's gaze squarely on his face. Dave had been a good friend to Peter years before at the time of his father's death. He was used to the manner in which the bishop gave his earnest, and often wise, advice. Instead, the bishop sat back in his chair and smiled.

Helen slipped small dishes onto the table.

Dave took a deep breath. "One of my priests was murdered last night."

Helen gasped and said, "Oh, I am sorry. Anyone we know?"

Dave shook his head. "I don't think so. He wasn't the most sociable of souls and the parish...well, it has some peculiarities..."

They waited for him to continue.

"It's a sensitive site, and there are..." Dave spoke carefully, "We were very happy keeping the place as a quiet backwater. The last thing we wanted was a violent incident and—God help us!—press attention."

Peter frowned and said, "Why are you looking at me like that?"

"I think I might have a job for you."

CHAPTER THREE

Early Tuesday morning

Peter arrived at the rectory still not sure how it happened. Did he really volunteer to camp out at a murder scene?

The cold and bored policeman walking up and down the street seemed glad of some company.

Peter greeted him. "Good morning! I'm Peter Trowbridge. I hope you're expecting me."

He nodded. "Can I see some ID?"

"Right. Here...and this is the letter from my uncle."

The PC nodded again, looking it over, and said, "That's fine, sir."

Peter looked toward the rectory's front door. "What...um...state is the place in?"

"Well, I know the forensic team has finished. The place is open for you again. Have you contacted the cleaning company yet?"

"What cleaning company?"

"Sorry, your responsibility, the cleanup."

Peter nodded and said, "That'll be why you're walking around out here and not inside making yourself coffee."

"Too right, mate. I don't envy you." He pulled a key on a length of string from his breast pocket and handed it to Peter.

"Right...thanks."

Peter took several deep breaths of cool morning air, put the key in the lock, and opened the front door.

The vestibule was dark; all the doors were closed. Only the window at the top of the staircase shone light. He shouldered his overnight bag and went upstairs.

He glanced first in the bathroom. The place was a mess, and he guessed it had been that way for decades. One bedroom was the late reverend's. It suffered from the same deep disarray. Peter closed the door on it.

The guest room was cleaner. There were sheets on the bed but dust on the pillows. Peter dropped his bag and sighed. The third room, next to the bathroom, was filled with boxes and bags. Peter couldn't tell if any furniture lay beneath.

He heard voices outside. Through the grimy window, he saw the PC talking with a bike messenger. Had Uncle Dave sent something round already?

As soon as Peter appeared at the door, the cyclist shouted at him. "Oi! You opening the church, or what?"

Peter immediately didn't like his tone. The messenger was tall and muscular but dressed in a skintight bright yellow suit with black accents. The color, Peter thought, undermined an otherwise imposing demeanor.

Peter shook his head. "Not planning to today, no."

The cyclist swore. "Where's Bart? Why can't I see him?"

Peter wasn't sure how to answer this. His uncle had said various things about not wanting a media fuss but hadn't specifically told him whether or not to talk about what had happened.

"There'll be an announcement. Can't say exactly when."

Turning his bike around and dropping it hard, the messenger swore again and launched himself off at high speed.

"Any idea what that's about?" Peter asked the policeman.

He shook his head. "Seen him around. Don't know what his business is here."

"You said something about a cleaning company. How do I contact them?"

The PC shrugged. "I know Detective Mason was put in charge. He's probably able to give you the details."

Peter looked at his phone. The time was seven forty-five. "Any idea when he'll be here?"

"I'm due off at eight. I suppose one of my colleagues will be assigned, just in case." He shook his head. "They didn't say anything more."

"Sounds like we're in the same boat."

Peter only looked in the kitchen once.

The downstairs room to the right of the vestibule was the parish office. On the walls was a haphazard rogues' gallery of former parish priests. Peter spent a few minutes watching the history of the church displayed in the faces of these men. He wondered at how much the world changed between the elderly Fr. Wilson during the twenties and the young Fr. Wilkinson during the Second World War, between the sour-faced Fr. Kowalik and the smiling post-Vatican-II Fr. Roberts. Despite the vastly differing circumstances of their times, they all heard and answered the call.

Peter shook his head. "No, I couldn't have done what you did."

Around the office, ancient filing cabinets creaked under imminent avalanches of paper. The front window looked out on the street, the park, and the hall. He hadn't noticed the building before, but the sign clearly stated "St. John's Parish Hall." It was squeezed between the tall shrubs of the park and the fence of the building site.

Peter sat in the chair behind the desk and sighed.

"Just keep the lights on, until I can get someone else in there," Uncle Dave had said. Sitting in a stranger's chair in a silent room, Peter had no idea what that meant.

The telephone erupted into a clamor. Peter stared at it, startled. "Hello?"

"Hey, Bart, Miles Treverton, *The One Daily.* So, yeah, what was the police activity at your place yesterday?"

Treverton's voice was quick and gravelly. Peter hesitated. "Um, this isn't Bart."

"Oh, right. Who are you then?"

"I'm Peter Trowbridge."

There was a moment's silence. "Who?"

"I'm...um...temporary caretaker."

"Oh, right. So what was happening?"

Peter felt a chasm open at his feet. "I'm not sure I can tell you anything right now. Sorry."

"Yeah? Okay, so what can't you tell me about?"

Peter didn't reply.

Treverton continued, "I mean, just give me the context, so I know what to ask for when I call back, okay?"

"I'm sure there'll be an announcement later," Peter said, sure now he was doing it all wrong.

"Great. Thanks! About what?"

Peter held the phone away from his face and looked at it. "That's all I can say."

"Oh, right. No, that's fine. That's fine. Your name again? Peter..."

"Trowbridge. Peter Trowbridge."

"And how long have you been housekeeper? Where did you come from?"

"I only..." He stopped himself. "That's all. Good day."

He hung up.

The phone rang again immediately.

"Hello?"

"Miles Treverton. We got cut off. You were saying..."

Peter hung up. He realized he was sweating. The phone rang. He looked at the caller ID. It showed "Treverton." Peter didn't answer.

He stepped outside to avoid hearing the phone ringing. He noticed the replacement police officer was sitting in her car at the end of the street. As he looked down the street, the side door of the church opened. A man descended the few stone steps and strode across the street into the park.

"Hello! Hey!" Peter called but received no acknowledgment or answer. The man hurried off through the park to the alley behind the pub.

Peter's phone vibrated in his pocket.

"Hello?"

"Peter! Uncle Dave. Are you in place?"

"Sort of. The press are calling already."

"I was afraid of that. Don't tell them anything."

"I don't think that'll stop them. Is there going to be an official announcement?"

"Work with the lead detective, Fred Mason, as far as that goes. Listen, I can't get there today. I've given your number to John Marx. He's a friend of mine and the vicar of St. John's On The Green. He'll be of most help to you in getting orientated, okay?"

"Wait, what was that?"

"He'll call you—John Marx. Talk to you later!"

Peter, becoming more angry than confused, turned back to the house. Before he got to the door, a car roared down the street.

As the passenger emerged, Peter instantly knew he was a detective. His suit had been a good one once. His shoes would probably still shine up with effort. But it wasn't his clothes that struck Peter most but the way he took a deep breath and straightened before looking up. He was like someone repositioning a heavy load. He guessed the man's graying hair wasn't an indicator of age.

"Mr. Trowbridge? I'm Fred Mason. I've been...er, given charge of this investigation. Your uncle told me you'd be coming."

"How do you do? I have a few questions to ask you."

"I'm sure you do." He glanced at the rectory. "Let's get a cup of coffee. There's a café just down from the pub."

Peter nodded.

* * *

The café was a throwback to before the days of coffee retail empires and loyalty cards. Its sign merely said "CAFE" and its smeared windows were clouded by steam. They sat at a Formica table, surrounded by the smell of toast and bleach.

Mason began, "What's your phone number? So I can text you."

Peter told him.

"Right. Thanks." Ripping packets of sweetener into his coffee, he asked, "So...what do you know so far?"

"That Fr. Samuels was murdered. I've seen the kitchen."

Mason nodded. "Beheading is rare. Bit of a first for us here."

"Uncle Dave talked about it being a sensitive...something or other. There's something about this place?"

"Everyone's on eggshells while the Islamic Centre goes up."

"Oh, is that what...?"

"Yeah, it's going to be their biggest mosque in London, university, library, who-knows-what. And St. John's is right up its backside."

"It is extremely close."

"Yeah, you want to watch out while you're here. We had a series of complaints from Fr. Samuels about them moving the construction fence. There's supposed to be an alleyway down the side of the hall. Someone's been pushing the fence up against the wall. It's the kind of stupid crap that can get out of hand."

Peter sighed. "I don't know how much help I can be with..."

"We don't want provocateurs saying the murder was anything to do with the Muslims."

"Oh, I see...I suppose they might."

"In a heartbeat, they will."

Peter sipped his coffee. "But, then, it might actually be...if there's been bad feeling."

Mason smiled. "The pathologist muttered something about 'less a machete more a ceremonial sword.' Some of them go in for that sort of thing."

"So...wait! You don't want anyone saying it's related to the mosque, but you're thinking it is."

"I'm going to have to investigate all the possibilities. The calmer the environment I get to work in, the easier it'll be."

"Right...best of luck."

"So, I'll be—I hope my team will be—talking to all the neighbors, interviewing all the parishioners, everyone who uses the church hall."

"Blimey! That'll be quite a list."

"Your uncle said you could help compiling the names."

Peter exhaled loudly. "I've seen the office. It isn't what I'd call organized. I'll do what I can." He nodded slowly. "Sure, that's something I can do."

"Good. Now, people will be coming and going, gossiping and talking," said the detective quietly, "I'd like to know what's being said. Know what I mean?"

"Keep my ear to the ground?"

"I can't be everywhere, and uniformed officers aren't most people's first choice to chat with. Your uncle's put you in pole position to hear what's being said."

Peter nodded but felt uncomfortable; Uncle Dave should have mentioned that part of it.

"There are some other little wrinkles in working on this," Mason continued.

Peter's phone vibrated. "Hold on a sec. Who's this?"

Mason waved for him to answer it.

"Hello? Sorry, who? Oh, right, yes, sorry. Uncle Dave said you'd call...right. At the church? I'm not there right now. Hold on." He held the phone away and said to Mason, "John Marx, a vicar, wants to see me. How long shall I tell him?"

Mason nodded his head and replied, "We can walk back now. I'll talk to him too."

"Oh...okay." Back on his phone, Peter said, "Two minutes. That alright? Okay."

They finished their coffees and set off toward St. John's. As they walked, Mason asked, "What do you know about The Ambulatory?"

"The what?"

"Ah, I see."

Peter waited.

"St. John's Ambulatory. It's...what is it? An architectural feature. Yeah, something like that. Bit unusual."

"Sounds like it should be a first aid center."

Mason laughed. "A lot of people think it is. But, no. It's a passage, a walkway."

"Oh."

"John Marx will probably take you through it."

"He will?"

"Yeah, I might come with you."

Peter suddenly remembered the kitchen and said, " Cleanup company. Your man outside said something about getting a company to clean up?"

"Oh, right. Yes. You should arrange that. I'll text you the details."

"Right."

There was no sign of anyone waiting outside the church.

"You have the keys?" Mason asked.

"No. Only to the rectory."

Mason walked down to his car, opened the trunk, and fished out a plastic bag. He took out a bunch of keys and flattened the bag on the roof of the car. "Sign here." He pointed to a writable area on the bag. "They're evidence."

"I suppose so..."

As they unlocked the side door of the church, Peter said, "Oh, earlier I thought I saw someone come out of this door and go across the park..."

Mason smiled and said, "Don't worry about it."

"Really? I thought you'd be interested in someone being inside the church."

"Yeah. You'll see."

CHAPTER FOUR

Tuesday morning

The interior of St. John's In The Green was brighter than its exterior suggested. The plain windows bathed the pews with a soft light and illuminated the woodwork dark with age and wear and the large statues looming in shadowed alcoves.

The altar was a plain marble rectangle several feet in front of a more elaborate carving of columns and marble angels—angels guarding the gold-plated, polished, and shining tabernacle.

Peter looked around for the sanctuary lamp. Half the candle was still burning. He faced the tabernacle and genuflected.

To either side of the altar was a door. On the right was a plain door, probably, Peter thought, to the vestry and then the rectory kitchen crime scene. On the left the door was open, but next to it was a large board. In an elegant script was written "Saint John's Ambulatory. No person shall enter here without permission. Instruction must be given. No child may enter."

At the bottom of the board was a motto in Latin, "Manusque murum semper." Underneath that was a piece of paper attached with pins: "The Archdiocese of Southwark is not responsible for any loss or damage incurred through the use of The Ambulatory. Those entering assume all risks to property and person."

"Want to have a look?" asked Mason.

Peter nodded.

The doorway opened to the top of a flight of stone steps, descending steeply. A bare light bulb, at the end of a run of ancient wire, clung to the wall above. The steps curved right, taking them down behind the wall of the altar, and then opened to another flight that turned left, putting the altar behind and some way above.

They descended to a circular room, its walls aged and damp.

Peter glanced at plastic tubs and loops of cables stored against the steps, but his attention was forward, drawn only to the large, dark mouth of a passage.

The opening was the size of a railway tunnel and edged in rounded stones. The passage floor was slate gray and smooth.

Out of the darkness of the tunnel came a short round man wearing a clerical collar. "Hello, Fred! And you must be Peter! I'm John Marx."

Peter was dumbstruck: by the tunnel mouth, by the smell, by the incongruity of this jovial man emerging from the darkness.

Mason laughed. "Don't worry. It takes a while to get used to it."

Peter gestured to encompass the tunnel, "What is this?"

Marx took his hand and shook it. "Don't worry, my dear fellow, all will be revealed. It was very bad of your uncle not to warn you. But, it's easily mended."

"It smells like a cave," Peter said.

"Oh, yes. Quite distinctive, isn't it? The smell of history, some call it."

Mason said to the vicar, "I'll need to get interviews going at your end. I'll come with you."

"Oh good, good! How's your wife?"

Mason nodded. "Doin' well, thanks."

The vicar put his hand on Peter's shoulder. "Peter, now listen carefully. When we go through The Ambulatory, there is a part where it's very dark. You must keep your hand on the wall and follow it round. Understand? You must, must keep in contact with the wall."

"What do you mean 'go through'? Where are we going?"

"Oh dear, yes. We're going to my church, St. John's On The Green. Remember, there's a dark part of the passage—hand on the wall at all times!"

"Okay..."

"Just like the signs say 'Manusque murum semper'!"

Peter had no idea what Marx meant.

The distinctive smell intensified as they stepped into the passage.

The vicar had him place his hand on the right-hand wall. The stone was smooth and seemed to glisten slightly.

They set off; the vicar in front, Peter in the middle, Mason following. No one spoke.

The wall curved gently to the right and the light from the circular room dimmed. Peter's eyes adjusted to pick up faint shapes. He could still see Marx's head and the curve of the wall. Where his hand stroked the stone, the wall seemed indented, as if a sculptor had taken pains to soften its vertical line.

After a short while, Marx said, "Here we go, hand on the wall, Peter." The vicar's voice seemed suddenly further ahead than the barely visible shape of his head.

At once Peter was aware of cold air to his left. He sensed the dark wall of the other side of the tunnel had given way to a huge cavern. The awareness of a vast expanse made him turn his head. He felt Mason's hand on his shoulder. His own hand had almost lifted from the stone.

As they walked, their steps were no longer echoing, the sound lost into the emptiness around them. The wall curved suddenly hard right.

Peter's head began to swim. The tight turn continued. He couldn't see anything ahead of him. He couldn't see the wall or his own hand. He stumbled but kept contact with the stone. The wall continued its crazy sharp turn; he felt he must surely be already walking back toward the circular room.

The turn continued.

They walked on. Peter began to lose any sense of direction or of how long he had been in the dark. Still the wall curved but then the path eased and straightened. He could see the round head of Marx, dim light in the distance silhouetting him. He could again hear Mason's footfalls behind him.

They emerged into a circular room. A stack of chairs and tables piled with colorful cloths confirmed it was not the room Peter had left.

"Okay, that was weird."

Mason chuckled and said, "Only a bit."

The vicar led them up similar but opposite sets of stone steps. Peter found himself in a familiar looking church, though this one had stained glass and red wood pews and smelled of polish.

"Welcome to St. John's On The Green!" said Marx.

"Wait! You're saying 'On The Green' not 'In The Green.'"

"Of course! Our two churches were built as mirror images of each other, at either end of The Ambulatory."

"Okay. So where are we?"

"Ah." The vicar smiled. "It's very simple: 'In the Green,' London; 'On The Green,' Manchester. You just traveled one hundred and sixty-one miles."

Mason smiled and said quietly, "Now that is the weird bit."

They led Peter to a pew and sat him down.

Peter coughed. "How...how long did that take?"

Marx smiled. "Oh, about four minutes."

Peter inhaled deeply, then said, "And people know about this?"

"Your uncle asked me to take you through and show you. The rest of the story you can pick up as you go. But, yes, people know about it. The Romans knew about it and built temples on either end, though, I understand, The Ambulatory predates them by a long way. I suppose we followed their example by building the churches on the same sites."

Mason said, "I need to get the Manchester force organized at this end. You'll be okay?"

Peter and Marx both nodded.

"Come along, Peter, my boy, I'll put the kettle on."

* * *

The vicar's rectory was of a similar size, though modernized and better furnished than Fr. Samuels'.

Over tea, Peter asked, "Why isn't this thing all over the news? I mean, at least, on the Discovery Channel, or something?"

John Marx sighed and said, "Well, it is quite well-known to academics. And our ufologist friends come back to visit when the skies disappoint. But, really, let's face it..." The vicar began to count on his fingers. "It isn't photogenic; it smells unpleasant; it's one of those things that has just 'always been there'; and, quite frankly, it is of limited utility. You can only transport what you can carry. A bicycle is as large a vehicle as will fit down the stairs or go easily around the curve."

"Why don't you take lights down with you?"

John shrugged and said, "They don't show you anything."

"Really?"

The vicar shook his head. "One of the many oddities. Turn a light to the left as it opens out and you can see a floor dropping away and no wall or roof, just darkness. At the turn, bulbs dim only to revive near the other end."

"Are scientists studying it?"

"Actually, yes. A group from Cambridge is just starting up another round of tests. Bart had seen them last week, I think. Isn't there a stash of equipment at your end?"

"Oh, maybe. Cables and tubs of gear..."

"That's them. Oh dear, they'll probably be knocking on your door in fairly short order."

"Mason will want to talk to them too."

"Ah, yes, about the matter at hand..."

Peter waited.

John continued quietly, "The matter at hand...As you'll soon hear, if you haven't already, Bart was a difficult man. He had very clear opinions, loved his church and its teachings. But by no means was he a 'people person.'"

"I've been getting that impression."

"He hated The Ambulatory. He would have filled it in if he could. He wanted nothing in his church that would distract his flock from the Lord. An admirable sentiment but, as he found, not a practical one."

"Who owns it?"

John laughed. "The Queen. Like swans, ownership defaults to Her Majesty. This church is owned by the C. of E., of course, for which you are quite entitled to blame the court of Henry VIII. But 'In The Green' is Catholic. It was transferred back to the Roman Church in some sort of backroom deal during the First World War. They swapped it for a hospital building or some such thing. The Dave would know better than I."

"Do you charge people to go through?"

"Oh heavens, no! What a legal quagmire that would be. Bad enough as it is if they should go missing."

"Go what? People go missing?"

John nodded. "Not always easy to tell if they just didn't come out, or if they never went in. We don't keep records. All part of not being seen to be in any way responsible."

"That's...disturbing."

"We don't promote The Ambulatory. But there are those who know. We have regulars commuting both ways to work every day. We haven't lost anyone in my tenure here, as far as I know, and I would certainly prefer to keep it that way. I can let you read some of the articles written by my predecessors if you like. The troubling stories tend to be the one-off visitors who went astray. Perhaps they let go of the wall..."

"What would happen?" Peter shuddered as he remembered what it had felt like hitting the sharp bend with the emptiness opening up around them.

John smiled grimly. "No one knows. However, the instructions have always been the same. They've found Roman, Saxon, and Norman inscriptions all saying the same thing. 'Keep your hands on the wall at all times': 'Manusque murum semper.' Did you not take Latin?"

Peter shook his head. "Wasn't required for my generation."

"Ah...pity!"

Peter thought for a while. "The fellow I saw coming out of the church this morning must have come through from here."

John nodded, "Probably."

"And the bike messenger couldn't get in because I hadn't opened the church up."

"Right. The few who used it regularly will get very vocal if you mess up their commute. Open the doors by six, I'd recommend."

"And close up?"

"I usually call time at ten thirty. Try to avoid the drunks on a dare."

"Oh God, I see what you mean."

"And watch young Sean and his bicycle. He's...a troubled young man."

"Seems to have a bit of an attitude."

"Hmm. I probably shouldn't say too much. Don't let him in the rectory. Suffice it to say that people would talk."

Peter shrugged. "Can I ask what Uncle Dave said to you about what I was supposed to be doing?"

"Hmm? Oh...not a lot. He said he was 'putting you in to keep the lights on.' I take that to mean to keep the commuters quiet; put the heating on, if the faithful need it; make tea for the visiting clergy..." John smiled mischievously.

"Oh...I see." Peter raised his teacup in salute. "I shall be happy to reciprocate. Which reminds me, Mason was supposed to tell me about a cleaning service."

"Ah, yes...And there may be a couple of parishioners you could call on for help with Bart's effects. I believe he had no family left."

Peter nodded and checked his phone. "Oh, he sent it already." He sighed and sat back from the kitchen table. "Thanks for the hospitality. I think I'd better get to work."

"Of course, my dear fellow. Do you...? Would you like me to come back with you?"

"Please. That journey...is going to take some...Yes. Please."

CHAPTER FIVE

Later Tuesday morning, lunch, and afternoon tea

John Marx worked wonders with the irate commuters locked out of In The Green. Peter learned the intricacies of the push bar locks, with their several settings all designed to frustrate everyone on both sides of the door.

As he returned to the rectory, the phone was ringing. It was Treverton, so Peter used his mobile to call the cleaning service. Soon after, there was a knock on the door.

Peter opened the door to find himself face-to-face with a teenager in a nicely cut coat and a cloud of cigarette smoke. Before Peter could speak, the boy threw his cigarette into the gutter and put his hand around the edge of the door.

"Treverton. What's going on?"

"Excuse me?" said Peter, bracing his foot against the inside of the door. He blinked twice at the incongruity of such an old voice coming from so young a face.

"Yeah, you're excused. What's going on? Where's Bart?"

"I've already told you there'll be an announcement."

"No, no, no." Treverton wagged his finger at Peter. "That ain't how it works. Bart always keeps me in the loop. We have a deal."

"Take your hand off the door, Mr. Treverton."

"Listen, matey, don't get off to a bad start here..."

Peter thought of the two brothers he had met in Nepal; one talked charmingly while the other lifted wallets. He had told himself then and told himself now, *Empathy, tolerance, and politeness all have their limits.*

Treverton yelled as his knuckles hit the doorframe.

"You bastard!"

Peter opened the door slightly and slammed it again. He called Uncle Dave.

"Hi, I think I just made a statement to the press."

* * *

The cleaners came quickly and started working. A parishioner called. Someone from a printing company called about the weekend bulletin. Another parishioner called. The dry cleaners called. Two parishioners knocked at the door. Eventually, Detective Mason came back.

"How's it going?" he asked.

Peter smiled and said, "When do you tell the press that something happened here?"

Mason smiled back. "I'm waiting for permission."

"From whom?"

"It's complicated."

"Word's out already."

"I know. We've already had a report from a Mr. Treverton of an assault on these premises."

"Really?"

"He won't press charges. The little oink knows we have too much on him."

"So, what happens? I presume the other papers will come sniffing. You can't keep it quiet."

"Give me a couple of hours. Like I said, it's complicated."

Peter shook his head dissatisfied. "These cleaners...Who pays for this?"

"Your insurance, usually. A question for your uncle."

Peter nodded.

Mason said, "I'll get back to you. Hang tight."

Peter retreated into Bart's office to continue the search for a parish register.

* * *

The cleaning team's head was a tall young woman, calling herself Boud. Peter immediately assumed her to be a hockey player, a horse enthusiast, and to have another name.

"Can I ask you something?" he said to her as she came back into the rectory from one of her trips to the large unmarked van.

"Of course, Mr. Trowbridge! How can I help?"

"Do you just do the...room itself? Could you see to the rest of the place, while you're here?"

"Well, what do you mean exactly?"

He showed her the bathroom upstairs and Bart's room.

"Not normally our bailiwick, I'm afraid."

"But could you stretch a point? I don't think there are any relatives, you see...and we have to keep the operation running here."

She shrugged her broad shoulders and said, "I can add it to the bill. You would need to sign that it was all authorized."

"Not a problem," Peter smiled. "Thanks, Boud."

* * *

After lunch at the café, Peter took a walk in the small park. His head was spinning from his morning wading through parish records, dealing with the noxious Treverton, and thoughts of that troubling passageway. He prayed he was doing okay.

He wondered why the druids who turn up at Stonehenge for the solstices and equinoxes weren't sitting smoking pot in The Ambulatory entrances. He smiled to himself. The normality of the churches and the comfortable urban lives of their clergy and parishioners might be all the protection the place needed. Despite the passage's unsettling atmosphere and remarkable function, here it was in the most nondescript street, under a church most would pass by and never notice. As much as he often chaffed against the church for not being radical enough, he could see a sense in which its consistency and mundanity could itself be a kind of witness against the wacky and the half-baked.

He walked to the end of the park where the fence was broken down at the back of the hall. A pile of trash spilled through the gap. As he looked, trying to work out what the trash was, he saw movement beyond on the other side of the construction fence.

A man in white was walking slowly between the scaffolding, his face down, talking quietly to himself. Peter thought, *Pakistani, maybe Afghani. Possibly the mover of the fence?*

"Hello!" He waved at the man but received no reply. Peter watched him as he walked behind a plastic-covered area of scaffolding. Maneuvering between buckets and rubbish, Peter moved up to the fence and slid between it and the wall of the hall all the way back to the road. He waited for his neighbor to pass by.

"Hello, neighbor!" he tried again.

The man nodded and said, "As-salamu alaykum."

Peter continued. "I'm staying here in the rectory. Are you involved in the building work here?"

The man nodded. "Yes, sir, I come to see our progress."

Peter, aware there had been no one working at the site all day, said nothing.

"I am Mufarrij. Who are you, sir?"

"My name is Peter. I'll be staying here for a while. Have you heard what happened here?"

Mufarrij tilted his head and waited. His clothes were immaculately white: the loose jacket trimmed with gold thread, the trousers, even his pillbox hat. He held a string of black beads in his right hand.

"I'm afraid Fr. Samuels is dead."

"Oh, this is sad news!" He put the beads into a pocket while giving Peter a sideways look. "Are you also a priest?"

"Um, no. I'm a sort of housekeeper."

Mufarrij nodded. "A sudden death challenges us. We are challenged to accept the will of Allah, Subhanahu Wa Ta'ala. We are reminded He is the Guardian and Disposer of all affairs."

"Indeed," said Peter, noncommittally. "Did you see Fr. Samuels often?"

Mufarrij flashed his eyes at Peter. "Oh yes, young sir, I saw him often. He was often at the fence here."

"I hope he invited you to tea in the rectory."

"Ah, such invitations...are beyond him, now."

Peter could read nothing from Mufarrij's remark. "But not beyond me. Give me a day or so to settle in and then I hope you will visit."

"Thank you. Thank you, sir. Good day." He waved his hand and walked on beyond a dragging plastic sheet and back under the scaffolding.

"Huh!" said Peter to the air. He had met few Muslims. Too few to be sure if he could trust when his instincts told him this fellow was odd. He was too well-dressed to come inspecting a building site and too polite to be a foreman. Peter noted the only question Mufarrij had asked was whether he was also a priest.

"Huh!" he said again.

As he turned back to the rectory, Mason returned. Accompanying him was a young woman in a dark green designer suit.

"Hi, I'm Peter," he said.

"I know," she replied with a smile. "Shall we go in?"

Peter glanced at Mason, who looked uncomfortable. *What*, Peter asked himself, *makes a detective chew his own lip?*

The kitchen was still a hive of activity. Peter uncovered two spare chairs in the office. The woman sat behind the desk.

"Now, Mr. Trowbridge, what have you said about Fr. Samuels' death and to whom?"

Peter tried to read what he could from her manner and appearance. Her hair was swept back and short. She wasn't as young as she first appeared. He tried not to dislike her, but she was being deliberately rude.

"Hello," he said, "My name's Peter. What's yours?"

She glanced at Mason, who sighed and said, "This is Fiona Chapman. I'm not at liberty to tell you which department she works for."

Peter laughed. "You are joking, right?"

Fiona wore no smile and Mason shook his head.

Peter laughed and swore at the same time.

"We think," Fiona began, "that the details of Fr. Samuels' murder should not be released. We will suggest natural causes pending further investigation and so forth. Who have you told so far?"

"I mentioned only that there would be an announcement...to an obnoxious teenager called Treverton of *The One Daily*. Oh, and to the bike messenger, I said the same thing."

"Next door?" she smiled softly, but Peter was aware she was watching him closely.

"I had a conversation with someone who seemed to be in charge. Polite, but cagey."

"And what did you tell him?"

"That Fr. Samuels had died suddenly."

"Nothing more?"

"Nothing more." Peter gave up all hope of ever doing anything but disliking her.

She looked at Mason, who it seemed to Peter, took it as a reprimand.

"You'll be telling me what this is about now," Peter said, more as a statement than a question.

"Perhaps. You come highly recommended by your uncle."

"That's nice. I used to think highly of him."

"And I believe your father's military service has some sway. Have you ever signed the Official Secrets Act, Mr. Trowbridge?"

"I don't think I've had the pleasure, no."

To Peter's utter disbelief she propped her briefcase up on the desk long enough to pull out a file. From it she pulled two sheets pinned together. "Sign at the bottom of page one and initial the box on page two. Put today's date in both places."

"Why?"

"Mr. Trowbridge, in your position as temporary caretaker of this property, I am forced to ask for your cooperation with an ongoing antiterrorism investigation, news of which—even of its existence— should it leak out, could compromise said investigation and possibly result in loss of life and or property. Put it this way, Peter, sign or immediately go back to being unemployed and living at your mother's."

"Oh well...I hadn't actually unpacked yet."

Mason interjected, "Look, Peter, we do need someone here. Your uncle's right, there has to be someone to keep the lights on. It can't be one of us. You're...explicable, explainable. It'll help a lot. Like I said before, people will talk to you when they won't talk to us."

Peter looked from Mason's face to Fiona's. "If I sign this, I could blurt out something unintentionally and end up in prison, right?"

Without any trace of emotion, she replied, "My argument against allowing you to remain at all is that you'll blurt out something and people will die."

"And I'd still end up in prison..."

"Your uncle highly recommends you, as I've said. Otherwise, I wouldn't even consider this arrangement." She waved the pages at him again.

Peter said nothing. Mason chewed his lip.

"Sign or leave, Peter. I can give you no more information without a signature."

"You'll tell me enough, so I don't say the wrong things...to the wrong people. I mean, you'll actually tell me what's going on?"

Fiona glanced at Mason again. "I'll have to, won't I?"

Peter swore and took the papers. He signed them and handed them back.

"Thank you, Mr. Trowbridge." She checked both pages and slid the signed pages back into the file and the file back into the briefcase, which she locked with a key.

She smiled at the two men and said, "Have the cleaners finished in the kitchen yet?"

"I don't think so," Peter said.

"I was going to ask you to make a cup of tea. Isn't there a café nearby?"

Mason smiled wryly. "Round the corner. Are you sure you want to be seen fraternizing?"

"Okay. For phase one, I am a financial auditor from the Archdiocese. That should prompt irrelevant questions as to whether there have been improprieties at St. John's to which the answer is 'it is purely routine.' Understood?" She waited until Peter nodded. "So, it's fine if we are all seen together." She paused and then asked, "Which room upstairs has the best view of the street?"

Peter thought, "You get an angle to the main road from Samuels' room...more mosque from the guest room."

She nodded and said, "Have the cleaners prep the guest room for me."

"You're...staying?" asked Peter.

"Of course."

"Oh...I'd been assuming I was in the guest room."

"Not squeamish, are you?" she shot back.

Peter shrugged.

As they left for the café, Mason caught Peter's arm, and they both fell behind Fiona. Quietly he said, "You did get that bit about making her tea, didn't you?"

"What?"

"She specifically meant you. You're the housekeeper, remember?"

"Oh shit..."

"Oh yeah, mate." Mason smiled. "Listen. We'll both be at this for a while. Call me Fred."

"Okay...Fred."

"Are you a Peter or a Pete?"

"Well, it's always been Peter."

Fred nodded. "Well, Peter, good luck with Ms. Chapman."

"Um...thanks. Looks like I'm going to need it."

CHAPTER SIX

Tuesday afternoon into Tuesday night

Good news came from the cleaners in the form of an open kitchen door. Bad news was in a note on the kitchen table.

"Guest room done. Out of time today. Rest of upstairs tomorrow. Boud."

Peter had come back to the rectory with Fiona. "Ah...," he said handing her the note.

She nodded. "So where will you sleep?"

"I suppose I'll change the bedding in Bart's room myself."

"Good man."

"This kitchen sink is now cleaner than the one in the bathroom."

The doorbell rang. Fiona disappeared into the scullery.

Two ladies of the parish stood at the door.

"Hello," said Peter.

"Yes...Hello, dear. We were looking for Fr. Samuels."

"I'm afraid I have bad news for you." Peter took a deep breath. "Fr. Samuels died Sunday night."

Both ladies gasped. "Oh, dear. How?"

"I'm afraid I don't know the details," Peter lied. "I was asked to step in and look after things by Bishop Davidson."

"Oh, will you be celebrating Mass?"

"Ah, no, I'm not a priest...Um, more a caretaker."

Both looked disappointed.

"Was there something specific you needed tonight?"

"Well, we have a meeting in the hall, you see."

"Okay." Peter waited.

35

"Fr. Samuels...would open up for us."

"Right! Okay. Yes...Let me do that straight away."

It took a while for Peter to work out which keys opened the hall.

The ladies turned on the lights, and he took a turn around the space. It was surprisingly large. The floor was clean, new hardwood.

A small scream from the kitchen made him run back from the middle of the hall, his footsteps echoing.

"What is it?"

"Those bloody Morris men! Look at this!"

The kitchen had been invaded by small casks of beer. Several were on the counters; others squeezed onto chairs. Each had a small tray under its spout, and each had its own covering of damp cloths.

"Morris men?" Peter asked.

"They come in here and...just look at it! What are we going to do now?"

"Did you need the kitchen for your meeting?"

"Well...we usually put some tea on."

Peter glanced around. There was a side table next to the fridge with an electric kettle, teapot, and a box of tea bags.

"Um, looks like someone's thought of that." He checked the kettle. "Can you manage with this?"

"Well, really! I'm surprised Fr. Samuels allowed all this sort of thing."

"I don't understand. Are the Morris men a regular thing?"

The woman's companion said, "Every week...since I can remember. Mondays, isn't it, Sue?"

"Well I don't hold with it," Sue muttered, "All them men wavin' hankies at each other. Who do they think they are?"

"Hello? Bart?" a man's voice boomed from the doorway. He was no taller than Peter but heavier, his face half concealed by a full black beard.

Peter stepped out to meet him. "Hello?"

"Oh, sorry," the man replied, "Is Fr. Samuels about?"

"I'm afraid there's bad news. Fr. Samuels died Sunday night. I'm Peter Trowbridge. The bishop asked me to step in as caretaker for a short while."

"Oh...Oh...I see."

Peter waited while the man thought, his eyes darting up and down the hall and to the kitchen.

"And you are?"

"Oh sorry, yes...I'm Jack—Jack Hadley—landlord of The White Hart, just round the corner."

"Ah, okay. So these are...," Peter indicated the barrels in the kitchen, "your doing?"

"That's right. Put them up last weekend. Check in every day. Got to be babied a bit, since the temperature in here gets a bit higher than I'd like."

Peter held up both hands to slow him down. "Um...why?"

Jack frowned in surprise. "For the feast. It's this weekend."

Peter frowned and shook his head.

Jack smiled. "Oh, my...timing is everything, isn't it? You say he died?"

"Late Sunday. What feast?"

"Morris Circle Feast. You've got a hundred and sixty, or so, Morris dancers in here Friday night to Sunday." Jack held up a finger. "There'll be six hired coaches lining up outside for the teams to go off touring the neighborhood, Saturday morning. But Friday and Saturday nights are my concern. They'll be drinking their way through as much beer as I can give 'em. Not just the men, mind you, the women's teams are fierce drinkers too!"

Peter blinked. "And this all had Fr. Samuels' blessing?"

Jack smiled again, "No, not exactly. His...last words...to me on the subject were 'Jack, I'm keepin' out the fuckin' way. There'd better be no trouble.' Not what I'd call a blessing, no." Jack moved into the kitchen with a nod to the ladies and began checking the casks. "He inherited the team practicing here from the former priest. Never liked it, but I think they pay good money for the rental." Jack stopped what he was doing. "He was alright last I saw him. It was some kind of joint practice; the lads were down from Trafford—Sunday that was—Bart locked up after 'em. What on earth happened to him?"

Peter shrugged and said, "Can't say. I only got here this morning."

"'In the midst of life we are in death' that's what he always used to say. Miserable bugger! Sad, though, to go so sudden...unprepared like."

Peter held his hands up to include the ladies and Jack. "I hope you'll all be able to manage in here at the same time."

Jack smiled and said, "I won't be a couple of minutes."

The ladies looked doubtful. Peter nodded to them and said, "I'm in the rectory when you want me to lock up."

"Bells, beards, and beer!" said Fiona with a smile, "All magnificently English."

"You knew about this, of course," Peter said.

She gave a quick nod. "Of course."

Peter scratched his head and said, "Bart had said he was going to keep out of the way. Any chance of me doing the same?"

"I think you only have to give them a set of keys to the hall and let them get on with it."

"Wait..." He thought for a moment. "The ladies said they practice on Mondays, but Jack said there were there on Sunday for something. Does Fred know that?"

"Oh yes, it means there would have been an ungodly number of people on the street before the murder."

"But it sounds like they got on okay with Bart."

Fiona smiled. "No one 'got on' with Bart."

Peter sighed and looked out the window onto the street and the hall. "It's going to be a zoo, isn't it?"

"Get your coat on, Peter. It's opening time."

"What?"

"The White Hart. Opening time. We need to go and establish our cover stories."

"Our what?"

"Where else do you plant information? Where people gather to gossip! You've met Jack, and that's a start. Now we have to be seen by the Chattering Classes."

"But mine isn't a cover story," said Peter.

To his confusion, Fiona smiled and looked at him, saying quietly, "Brilliant!"

Under a sign depicting two young white deer, The White Hart was bigger than Peter had first noticed. It occupied half the block, the park and the hall being the other half. The front entrance on the corner was like the doorway of a small shop. Once in the vestibule one took the door to the left for the Pump Room. The door to the right led to a corridor down to the Lounge. The dark wooden staircase led up to the Tap Room.

In the Pump Room, both the drinking and the conversation were public affairs. The room had plain wooden furniture, an open feel now that cigarette smoking was banned, and no jukebox or television. It was a room that had successfully resisted change for nearly a century. Here, a cohort of scientists from nearby university and research buildings often regaled each other and any stray drinkers with long tales of bizarre oddities in their fields.

The Lounge was carpeted and quiet, more suited to private conversations. A low level of background noise came from the jukebox next to the bar and the chuckling robot-noises of two fruit machines. On a summer's night, the windows were opened onto the park to catch the sunset glow and wafts of fresh evening air.

The Tap Room at the top of the stairs stretched all the way to the back of the building and over both the Pump Room and the Lounge. It was a dance hall, disco party room, and concert hall. If the lower bars were too full, Jack would open it up to relieve the pressure. On the occasional night when the fine print of the licensing laws might dampen an otherwise marathon session, Jack would close the downstairs, lower the lights in the Tap Room, and carry on.

The Green Morris team split their Monday evenings equally between energetic dancing in the hall and well-lubricated singing in the Tap Room. It was also a tradition that had successfully resisted change for many decades.

Fiona's mission, to be seen and thereafter talked about, made the Pump Room the best choice.

As soon as she mentioned she was an archdiocesan accountant, Jack was on the bait like a terrier. "Things not all kosher at St. John's then?"

"I should hope not!" Fiona smiled. "You know I worked with an Israeli once, who gave me the inside scoop on the modern kosher observance."

"Oh yeah?" said Jack.

"Three fridges." She held up three fingers and checked that two regulars at the bar were watching and listening. "One for the meat, one for the milk..." She kept them waiting a second. "One for the non-kosher foods!"

"Ha!" Jack laughed. "I'll have to remember that one!" Then he immediately leaned over the bar toward Fiona and asked, "So you're here for the accounts—what?—at the request of the bishop, I suppose?"

"It's purely routine." She smiled and sweetly sipped her Guinness.

Peter and Fiona staked out a small table near the door and retreated there as the Pump Room filled to capacity. Fred Mason joined them. "Thought I might find you here."

"You meet the best sort here," Fiona replied with a smile.

To Peter he said, "You over your shock from this morning?"

Peter frowned and tried to think.

Fred prompted, "The Ambulatory?"

"Oh God! Was that only this morning?"

They all laughed.

Fred said, "Yeah, been a day, hasn't it?"

Peter shook his head and said, "Didn't know quite what Uncle Dave was getting me into..."

Fiona asked quietly, "Any leads?"

Fred shook his head. "With a field this broad, it'll take a while to shake out the threads."

Peter asked, "Don't you usually start by asking if the victim had any enemies?"

Fred and Fiona both laughed.

"Yeah, well," Mason replied, "You never met him, did you."

Peter smiled and said, "My uncle told me a bit. Jack actually said more. 'Miserable bugger' was the phrase. Not the usual description of a dearly departed."

Fred nodded. "But accurate. I haven't heard anyone yet with a good word to say about him."

"I'm sure he had some fans amongst the ladies of the parish," Peter said.

"That may be. I think there was a fairly consistent crowd on a Sunday."

"That would be 'congregation,' Inspector," Peter corrected him.

"Yeah, right. Whatever."

Peter glanced from one to the other. "My guess is neither of you are churchgoers?"

Fiona took a drink. Fred looked around at the bar and muttered something unintelligible.

Peter nodded and toasted the air between them.

* * *

Peter assumed Fiona was already in bed and asleep when he returned on his own from the pub several pints the better.

He stood in the bathroom noticing things: his pupils, slightly dilated; the thick stain around the sink that the cleaners would have trouble eradicating; Fiona's cosmetics bag; his own towel hanging on a hook, out of place in this foreign room; the tile work absent all artistry or charm; the sadly faded shower curtain around the unsightly bathtub; the silence.

It was the silence that put a chill into his heart. Just as he had stood before the impossible quiet of The Ambulatory, he stood before the silence of this bathroom. All Bart's years here, an unchanging sequence of nights alone, of set routines, like a repeating image of a mirror in a mirror. This was unlike the poverty Peter had feared if he had become a priest. This was worse than lack of money.

He wondered how Bart had faced it, what the priest did to get through. He thought, too, of his own father. What was it he saw—his last night—that made him choose to have no morning? What life could he have foreseen for himself that was so much worse than this life of Bart's? How bad does it have to get to shoot yourself?

The main ceiling light in Bart's room had a dim bulb. The piles of junk, clothes, papers, and books rivaled the mess of the office.

Peter looked into the wardrobe, glanced under a chair, opened some of the drawers. He found the largest, bottommost drawer locked.

"Huh! Who were you keeping things locked up from?"

He sat on the bed for a while, thinking how unlikely it was that he would sleep.

CHAPTER SEVEN

Wednesday morning

Peter almost fell down the stairs, thoroughly disorientated, as the knocking continued. He staggered into the vestibule and pulled the front door open.

"Ugh?" was the best he could manage.

The postman gave a cheery smile. "Good morning, sir! For the Reverend Samuels. Is he at home?"

Peter shook his head. "Deceased. Need a signature?"

"Oh...no, no, not necessary...Sorry to hear it. That does explain my not being able to deliver the last couple of days, what with the police and all."

The postman turned to his bike and unhooked a large plastic bag, full of mail. "There you go, sir."

"Thanks..." Now more awake, Peter asked, "Why do you knock? Why not put it through the letterbox?"

The postman pointed to the door and the steel plate fixed over the letterbox.

"What the..."

"The reverend gentleman had that done about a year ago."

"Why?"

He shook his head. "I'm sure I couldn't say, sir. But I understand he was quite insistent. We try and oblige when we can."

Peter shook his head. "Thanks, I'm sure I'll hear all about it eventually." He held up the bag of letters and said, "Thanks."

He was about to shut the door when Fiona appeared, crossing the street from the park. She was in another tight, dark business suit, as well turned out as the day before, despite the improvised arrangements of the rectory accommodation.

"Morning, Trowbridge!" she called.

"Mmmf!" Peter yawned in reply.

"Not a morning person I see."

"Coffee…"

"Well, that's a motive for you to explore the mysteries of Bart's kitchen!"

She threw several newspapers onto the kitchen table, sat down bolt upright, and began speed reading them.

Peter worked around her. There was coffee; life was good.

While the coffee brewed, he sat with one of the lowerbrow newspapers. A headline read "Tramps Injured by Knife-wielding Transvestite."

"How do they make this stuff up? And so consistently?"

Fiona didn't look up from her paper, but said, "What have you got?"

Peter read aloud: "'Homeless residents of Clifton Street reported being attacked by a man dressed in a skirt. No one could understand him' and…blah, blah…'wielding a large knife…ran off into the night.' Take out the hyperbole and that's all they've got. So the headline 'Tramps Injured by Knife-wielding Transvestite' is, actually, a good summary of what follows."

Fiona, still reading said, "Hmm, not a Scotsman then?"

"Maybe! The skirt and the foreign bit would fit. Is knife work native to the northern borders?"

"No, they do it with bagpipes. Coffee ready?"

The cleaners returned. Fiona moved into the office.

"Peter?" she called.

"Fiona."

"I'd like you to talk to our neighbors at the building site."

"Um, okay…"

"I'd like you to ask when they think the building work will get under way again."

"When did it stop?"

"Last week. We don't know why. I don't like not knowing things."

"I got the impression it's taking a long time to complete."

She nodded. "Many delays. Many changes to the plans. Many disputes between cousins and brothers-in-law—the work is mainly being kept in the extended family. This last stoppage is a little odd. Go and see what you can find out."

Peter shrugged. "I'll see what I can do." He looked at his phone. "Oh God, is that the time? I should have opened the church by now!"

"You just can't get the staff, can you?" she joked.

He squinted at her. "Haven't you got some accounts to audit?"

A small crowd waited for him at the church door. He smiled and bluffed his way through. "Morning all! Have you opened up in a jiffy!"

The bike messenger, still in yellow, said, "They're saying Bart's dead, is that right?"

"Um, yes. I'm afraid so."

Peter heard him catch his breath, then swear.

As he pulled the door open, Peter stood in the gap and turned to them all. "Just so you all know, Fr. Samuels died on Sunday night. I don't have any more details, I'm sorry. I'll be here for a while to open up and lock up at the usual times. If you haven't already spoken with the police at this end, you'll probably be contacted by someone from Manchester."

"Why are the police involved?" the messenger asked.

Peter shrugged. "Couldn't say."

As the crowd followed each other into the church and down the stairs to The Ambulatory, Peter listened. Everyone agreed that, if the police were involved, there must have been foul play.

He went down with them and watched as one by one they disappeared into the dark. After five or six were in and a couple were standing chatting, a woman walked out of the tunnel mouth.

"Morning!" she said to them. To Peter she said, "You're new. Or are you the caretaker chappie?"

Peter nodded and said, "Caretaker chappie. You've heard the news about Fr. Samuels?"

She nodded and said, "Sad. Not surprising. Sad though."

Peter asked, "Can I ask you something?" She nodded. "When you pass someone coming the other way...," he pointed back into The Ambulatory, "what happens?"

She laughed and shook her head. "You don't. You never see

anyone coming the other way. Never hear anyone either."

"Huh! How about that..."

"Bye now!"

Peter nodded. "Thanks!"

He heard the woman's voice again as she reached the top of the stairs. There followed two new voices and the banging of metal against the stonework.

"Oh shit! Who made these stairs so damn steep?" said the older voice.

"They outsourced it," said the younger voice.

Peter watched in some amusement as the pair erupted into the circular room both weighed down with metal briefcases, toolboxes, tripods, and other gear. They immediately piled it all on top of the tubs laid out to the left of the stairs.

The older man had a thin comb-over, a round face, and the shabby clothes of an academic. Rolling the stiffness from his shoulders, he looked around and saw Peter watching them.

"Shit! Who are you?"

The younger man, with a round oriental face and more fashionable attire, looked over his shoulder but said nothing.

"I'm Peter Trowbridge, temporary caretaker. Who are you?"

"Caretaker? Where's Bart?"

Peter looked from one to the other. "I'm sorry to have to tell you, Bart died, Sunday night."

"What of?"

"I couldn't say. I was asked to step in to keep things running."

"Shit, that puts us in a sticky position, doesn't it?"

Peter said, "Excuse me?"

The younger man spoke up. "Our arrangements were made with Bart himself we understand, to run some tests on the tunnel. I don't know if there was ever anything in writing."

Peter shook his head. "Don't worry, I know about that. I was expecting you."

The older man sighed and said, "Oh...well, okay. That's good. Died, you said? Any idea what happened?"

Peter shook his head. "Please, call me Peter. I'm staying in the rectory if you need me. You didn't tell me your names."

"Stephen. Doctor Stephen Wallace, Cambridge. Though, as Brad said, our funding isn't through our college..."

"I'm Brad. I'm one of the professor's assistants."

Given the fellow's obviously oriental features and accent, Peter was sure 'Brad' was a name assumed for the benefit of westerners.

"Well, good to meet you both. I hope we'll get some time to talk about what you're doing. I find this—all this—fascinating. I can't believe it's not more widely known."

The professor didn't smile. "It's a scandal. The church has sat on this for centuries! Well, that's going to change."

"I hear Bart didn't really approve of The Ambulatory."

Stephen nodded. "Tried to have it filled in a couple of times. There was always the risk he'd trap someone inside. That's really what stopped him. I suspect what persuaded him to let us in was the thought we might find a way to do it safely."

Brad said, "You're a priest, right?"

"Um, no. No, I'm just a caretaker."

"Sorry. I assumed you were. I mean you have that look about you."

"Really?" Peter replied noncommittally.

The professor turned and picked up a coil of cable. "You're at the rectory you said?"

Peter nodded.

"We'll catch up with you there...or at the pub more's likely."

Peter smiled and accepted his dismissal.

* * *

Rather than go back into the rectory, Peter walked over to the hall. The fence was up against the wall of the hall, where the day before he had walked easily between them. There was no sign of any activity beyond the fence, but as he turned to go back, a voice called, "Ah, Mr. Peter!"

Mufarrij appeared from behind some hanging plastic. He was not alone. The boy next to him seemed nervous, and Peter thought too young to be dressed in the same formal outfit as the older man.

"As-salamu alaykum," they both said.

"How are you today?" Peter asked cheerily.

"We are well, thank you. Please, Mr. Peter, meet my student, Ali."

"Hello, Ali."

The boy nodded twice but didn't say anything.

"How goes the work?" Peter asked with a look over their heads.

Mufarrij tilted his head and smiled. "The work goes on, whether brick-by-brick or heart-by-heart. The work of Allah The Magnificent and Most Blessed is not stopped."

"Of course," Peter smiled back, "but it must be frustrating to have to deal with delays in completing the building."

"If we meet an obstacle, sometimes the best response is to go around it."

The boy said something Peter didn't catch, and Mufarrij snapped back at him. Turning again to Peter he said, "What of your church, now the priest is gone? Will it close, as so many of your churches have closed?"

Peter thought, *Oh, here we go!* but said, "No, I think not." There was a short moment of silence; then Peter had an idea. "Um, if it did, would you be interested in buying it?"

Mufarrij shrugged and said, "Land in London is expensive, you know. But to have more space here might be something we should consider. Yes, Mr. Peter, perhaps it would be a blessing for all."

"Of course, you would have to take over The Ambulatory."

The boy's face flashed with fear. Mufarrij's eyes narrowed. "That thing is the devil's! Do not go in there, Mr. Peter! Nothing good can come from it. I spoke of it to your friend—many times! He and I agreed in that. He knew...he knew it was not good. Do not go there!"

This is interesting, Peter thought. He said, "Thank you for your concern. I have no plans to make regular use of it, though I see a group of people go through every day."

"Fools! Do not be like them!"

"Okay, but I don't see it doing them any harm."

Mufarrij raised a warning finger to Peter. "There is good and evil in our world. You know this! This thing exists to deceive, to take the mind away from true belief."

"I'm not sure I understand."

Mufarrij shook his head. "The path of true belief is clear before us. Those so-called scientists in there," he gestured toward the church, "try to convince us that Allah, Blessed be He, is an illusion. They lie!"

"Perhaps. But it would be good to know more about The

Ambulatory, wouldn't it?"

"No! Do not go in it! You, I hope, are wiser than that. Peace to you!"

Peter nodded, and the pair walked away in animated but whispered conversation.

* * *

Back in the rectory, all was quiet.

"Fiona?"

"One minute!" she called from her room upstairs.

Peter hunted for something to eat in Bart's cupboards.

"How did it go?" she asked as she stepped into the kitchen.

"Weren't you listening?"

"How would I do that?"

"Oh, I don't know. Long-range microphone, devices hung on the fence. How would we, mere citizens, know what you get up to?"

She paused before replying. "In this case, I was employing your ears rather than electronics. You can tell me what he said well enough."

"But you were watching."

"The angle was wrong. Couldn't see a thing."

"He wouldn't say a word about the building work. He'd love it if we closed up shop and sold the land to them."

"Interesting."

Peter sat down and thought. "Can I ask you a question?" Without waiting he went on. "Does The Ambulatory go right underneath the building site?"

Fiona sighed wearily and sat down. Peter was surprised and a little relieved to see some signs of emotion in her face.

"That thing is the bane of my life. It would appear from the position of the entrance that, yes, it goes directly under the neighboring property. The circular entrance room is directly under us here in the rectory. The beginning of the curve and the opening of the...expanse—or whatever it is—feels like it should be under where the actual mosque is being constructed in the center of the property. That, though, is as far as anyone can tell me. Ground-penetrating radar can't see it. Seismography didn't tell us anything. I've had the local water authority dig sideways out of the sewer right next to it, and they found nothing but dirt. It's as if it doesn't exist."

"Really?"

"But it wasn't doing any harm...except giving a few boffins sleepless nights. It's been there for centuries! Who cared that no one understood it? It was like Morris dancing, I suppose, it was one of those Great British Eccentricities. And then along they came...to build a bloody great mosque over it. Suddenly we have to care."

"That reminds me, Professor Wallace arrived."

Fiona nodded. "Just what we need, more bodies bumbling around."

CHAPTER EIGHT

Wednesday lunch into Wednesday night

Fred Mason appeared again after lunch.

"We have to announce it today," he said, accepting a mug of tea from Peter.

"Good," Peter replied, "I'm fed up obfuscating. People are funny the way they react, but it is bad news for them and, you know, bad news is bad news. I hate lying in such circumstances."

The detective pulled out a single sheet of folded paper.

"'Monday morning...'blah, blah...'Fr. Bartholomew Samuels was found dead in the rectory of St. John's In The Green. We are investigating the circumstances of his death. It appears an intruder, possibly an opportunistic burglar, was interrupted by the victim. Fr. Samuels had no next of kin.' That's it."

Peter asked, "Any ideas yet who your 'opportunist burglar' might have been?"

Fred shook his head. "Waiting on the Path lab, I need to hear what they say about the weapon. As for suspects...," he laughed, "I haven't met anyone who liked him, had a good word to say about him, or as far as I can tell, would have actually done the old sod any harm."

Peter said, "I heard that the neighbors might like to buy the property should it become available."

Fred looked doubtful. "If it was known that the place was certain to go on sale, maybe I'd have something to go on." He shook his head again. "Too tenuous."

"Just saying what I heard."

"No, no. Thanks, it's helpful. Keep listening."

Peter asked, "What's with the letter box being sealed up?"

Fred laughed and shook his head. "I read about that in the file. They never found out...maybe local kids. Who knows? One of the beat officers thought Bart was just being paranoid. Well, we know he was an odd man."

* * *

Fiona and Fred left together. Peter opened every kitchen cupboard and made a shopping list. He opened the fridge and threw out much of the contents. "Now, when do I put you out to be collected?" he asked the bin.

He walked down to the main street, passed by the pub, the Tandoori Palace, and the bathroom showroom. The traffic was heavy, but there were few pedestrians. The Tesco Express was happily empty of customers and the owner greeted him with a nod. Peter considered asking him about the mosque, but thought better of it.

As he came back toward The White Hart carrying his grocery bags, he noticed two men leaning against a bike rack. The pavement was wide enough to avoid getting too close. One man, sporting old, stale-looking tattoos, jeans, and work boots. His companion, wearing a "British Defense" muscle shirt, was otherwise dressed identically. Both had hair cropped into nonexistence. They pulled on their cigarettes and watched Peter approach.

Peter looked ahead and walked by.

"Oi, Bag-boy! Ain't ya got a woman to do that for ya?" said one. His friend laughed.

Peter walked on, passed the pub, and rounded the corner.

A voice followed him. "Poofter!"

"Nice neighborhood...," Peter muttered.

As he opened the rectory door, he glanced back along the road. The skinheads had moved to lean against the park fence and were watching him.

* * *

Peter bashed his grocery bags against the wall as he negotiated the front door. He had the door keys in his mouth as he stepped into the kitchen.

"Hello, Dear! Do you need my help with those?"

He stood staring at the silver-haired old lady sitting at the table, a pastry half-consumed on the plate before her.

"Mmmf!?"

"Well, I'm sure you're doing your best." She got up and took one of the bags from him.

He ripped the keys from his mouth and said, "Who are you?"

She nodded and put the bag on the table. "There now. Would you like a custard tart? Fr. Samuels loved them. I know they're not everyone's taste, but he liked them."

"What are you doing here?"

She looked up at Peter with clear gray eyes. "My Dear, it is you who is the stranger here, not I. Sit down. The kettle is ready to boil."

Peter held his tongue. While he stuffed his purchases into the fridge and cupboards, he watched her out of the corner of his eye as she made tea.

She was perhaps five feet tall, but her back was straight and her movements showed no sign of tremble or weakness. Age showed in her face, not her body.

She placed the teapot on the table, herself in the chair, and smiled.

He sat and said, "I'm Peter Trowbridge. I'm here as temporary caretaker in the aftermath of...Fr. Samuel's sudden departure."

"Oh, I dare say that's a good idea!" she replied. "I understand there is no longer such a wide stable of priests upon which to draw, in such circumstances, as once there was."

"And you are?"

"You can call me 'Ellie,' Dear."

Peter waited, his eyes on hers.

She reached for the milk and blinked. "I came regularly to see Fr. Samuels. He and I had much in common." With a conspiratorial glint in her eye, she added, "The Ambulatory is such a wonder, isn't it?" She poured milk into his cup.

"So, you are a friend of Bart's..."

Ellie smiled and said, "Perhaps a little strong a word. He was an irascible old coot but, perhaps, that's why I liked him. I have no time for glad-handers and salespeople. I'd rather you tell me that you don't trust me and throw me out than pretend to be polite—even if I have made you the best cup of tea you will have had in several days."

Peter smiled, then laughed. "I have no reason to either trust you or throw you out...yet. I probably do have the authority to do the latter, and we'll see when the tea brews. But, thank you."

"You're welcome."

"Had you seen Bart recently?"

"No. I live out in the sticks—as they say, all hay bales and hog stench. I treasured my trips into the city and my visits here. They were...nice."

"But you are here because you heard what happened?"

She nodded. "Yes, some friends let me know. I came at once. It's so unlikely that someone would have—as Elisa Doolittle might put it—'done the old boy in.'"

Peter nodded. "I understand the police are pursuing the idea of an opportunistic burglar." He bit into the custard tart.

Ellie fixed him with a steely glaze again. "The pub has money, the church has precious little, Fr. Samuels even less. No, not any sort of burglar I've met. There's a mystery here, Mr. Trowbridge, as big as that wonderful hole in the ground below our feet."

"You know much about The Ambulatory?" Peter asked, with an air of innocence.

Ellie laughed. "Oh yes. That's why I first came here. That's what Fr. Samuels and I would talk of long into the evening. It's the most remarkable structure, of such profound implications for physics, history, and yet..." She looked into the distance and sighed, "It is also profoundly disappointing in almost every way imaginable! Almost impervious to experimental investigation; dark; smelly; and of course, takes one from one dull corner of England and dumps one in another equally dull. The only mercy it shows is in doing it quickly!"

She smiled and her eyes sparkled at Peter with the fun of it.

Peter finished his tart and asked, "What do you think its history is?"

Ellie answered as she stirred the tea and poured it. "Your Roman forebears would have worshipped at its entrances. They were quite at peace with the idea of gods being in possession of places—and people. I think it predates them by many centuries, but it's hard to tell. Its otherworldly aspects for us, of course, would not have been otherworldly to them, just another part of the wonder of this world!

They would have respected it though, which, alas, Fr. Samuels never did. He feared it and feared anyone who came to investigate it."

"I don't see why he would have felt that."

"Remember, dear, he was employed by the church, with responsibility to ensure his flock neither fell to a competing theology, nor heard anything that might sow confusion in their minds. He could neither explain it in the light of scripture nor of tradition. Therefore, it must be of the devil."

"Ah..."

"Many nights I tried to open up his mind to the scientific approach to it, but I don't know how far I got. And now, of course..."

Peter was silent, trying to imagine how this slight old woman could maintain such a long debate with someone as renownedly ill-tempered as Bart.

Ellie continued. "There are some blurry markings just inside this end that some say represent Hecate's wheel which would put it fairly early. I think the Romans would have relished the primal feminine qualities of The Ambulatory; it's as a stark a stone vagina as I've ever seen." She winked at Peter, "Don't give me that shocked schoolboy look! You can be sure it's been the site of many a fertility ritual through the years." Then she wagged her finger at him saying, "Now, you know, of course, if The Ambulatory smelled of roses, and we painted the entrance pale blue, your uncle could pass it off as another miracle from the Blessed Virgin, perhaps graced to the world to...to do what might we say? Allow her pilgrims to process from one shrine to the next?"

Again, Peter saw her eyes twinkle, her face alive with mischief.

Peter flashed his eyes back. "Then, I suppose, neither the pub nor the church would suffer a lack of money."

Ellie chuckled, and they toasted each other with tea.

After tea, she stood to leave. "It was quick work by your uncle to put you in here so soon. Not many clergymen are that efficient."

"That's my Uncle Dave."

"I underestimated the man, something I rarely do."

Peter frowned.

She continued. "I'll be back to visit again. There will be things we need to discuss."

55

Peter didn't know what she meant, but smiled and nodded politely.

* * *

When Ellie had left, and the cleaners were done upstairs, Boud presented Peter with a large, heavy bag of magazines.

"What's this?"

"There's a saying in our work, Mr. Trowbridge, about the dead having no privacy. This lot was in a locked drawer. I presumed it should be opened."

"Okay..."

"Now, it's not unusual to find a stash of magazines in a deceased gentleman's room and, honestly, we pay little attention, but I've never seen treasures like this before, at least not locked so carefully away."

Peter glanced at the first cover: *UFO Omnibus,* Vol 6.

"Oh...I see..."

"Don't worry, we're under strict instruction from Detective Mason as to what's evidence and what isn't, and he says these are all yours. Happy reading!"

Her hearty laugh echoed back from the front door.

* * *

In the early evening, Peter went to the circular room to visit the scientists. No one was there. He stood in front of The Ambulatory opening. The smell of ages wafted out from the gloom. He listened, hearing behind him the traffic on the main road and a plane on its descent. No sound came from the tunnel. He felt the hairs on the back of his neck rising and the skin on his arms raising in goose bumps.

"This was here when Jesus was born. People walked into this then with as little idea of what it is as we have. God, what have you done here? What is this thing?"

He turned away and went to The White Hart.

Dr. Wallace and his assistant were at a table in the Pump Room, eating.

"Hi, may I join you?" Peter asked.

"Oh, hello again. Please." Wallace gestured to a chair.

"Thanks. How was your day?"

The two glanced at each other.

Wallace said, "Frustrating. But that's normal."

"Anything I can help with?"

He shook his head. "You can buy us more cable. I've laid out all we have and...I don't know..."

"What's the cable for?" Peter asked.

"Oh, we're installing cameras," said Wallace with enthusiasm, "It's a sort of CCTV for the tunnel. We'll space them out as far as we can, and..."

Brad finished the thought. "Watch the people come and go."

Peter thought for a moment. "How far is it to the crazy bend?"

Both men looked into their beer glasses.

"Hmm...not sure. We haven't got that far, " Wallace admitted.

"Wait, isn't that the first thing to do? I mean, start by measuring it?"

Wallace looked uncomfortable.

Brad stepped in. "That's just one of the interesting things about the project. Accurate measurements are problematic. Historically, no one's been able to record much by way of reliable data. Rather than rehash previous work, our idea is to start from a different point of view."

"We know," Wallace jumped in, "that people can see a fair bit during their way through. They see each other, even though it's dim. You can tell there's someone in front of you..."

"So," Brad continued evenly, "we want to start with what they see. Put our digital eyes up against the wall...regular video, then infrared, ultraviolet..."

"Sounds interesting." Peter nodded, encouragingly.

Brad shrugged. "We just hope the cameras last long enough."

"What do you mean?"

Brad stopped. Wallace coughed. Peter looked from one to the other.

Wallace said quietly, "Electronics are suspect in there. It's a hostile environment. Not sure why yet."

Peter frowned. "My phone didn't seem to mind."

Wallace shook his head. "Things fluctuate randomly. Different devices have different results. I fear that any lengthy exposure and they'll be toast."

"Really?"

Peter excused himself and went to the bar; the hairs on his neck were at it again.

Peter didn't notice exactly when and how the conversation had spread from just the three of them to the whole of the Pump Room. Theories were soon flying like paper planes around the assembled boffins.

One middle-aged academic cornered Peter at the end of the bar and softly insisted, through a haze of brandy fumes, that there was a black hole somewhere in the Midlands.

"Um...wouldn't that implode the Earth?" Peter asked.

"It hasn't yet, no...But think about it! Space-time is being warped. Somehow, they contained the distortion into a kind of string...the tunnel! Two strings, actually!"

"Two?"

"There and back again. You put your right hand on the wall going up to Manchester, don't you?" The man held up his right hand and swayed a little on his barstool.

Peter nodded. "Yeah."

"And when you're coming back?"

"The same."

The man shook his head. "Should be the left, if it's an ordinary tunnel. So, see, it must be a different wall. It's two paths through. One going one side of the anomaly perhaps and one the other. And no one is looking at how it was done! Once you're inside, it's no good..." He glanced at Wallace. "They'll never find anything inside. You have to look for the actual nexus point. Find out where in the Midlands to start digging, you see?"

Peter nodded politely. No, he did not see.

Another voice rose above the chatter assuring his listeners that they had never actually been through it. The Ambulatory was merely a shared hallucination, derived from a social and psychosexual construct.

* * *

Back from the pub, Peter sat on the bed leaning against the pillow and the wall, Bart's magazines slipping into a tide down the bedspread.

"Bart, Bart, Bart...What was all this? You were a reasonably rational, educated man! How could you read this drivel?"

Peter tossed an issue of The UFO Conspiracy onto the floor and picked up a new one. A photograph fell out.

It was almost completely black. A blur of movement crossed one corner.

Peter thought for a moment it was a piece of Bart's rubbish, but then remembered it had been in the locked drawer. He carefully raised the magazine by its spine and shook. Three more photographs fell out.

Two were similarly blurred and incomprehensible. The third was clear, although still suffering from low light. It showed a standard alien from the artwork in the magazines: rounded head; large, black, oval eyes; dots for a nose; a thin mouth; large fingers on small hands at the end of scrawny arms. The creature was standing before the silhouette of a large man. The man was odd in that he had some sort of rounded spike coming out of the top of his head. Peter saw, in the silhouette, a tinfoil hat.

"So which of these is you dressed up, Bart? And who's your friend?"

Peter reached over to the nightstand and tucked the photograph into his wallet. Maybe his uncle should see it; maybe he shouldn't.

* * *

Later, while down in the kitchen for a glass of water, he noticed a note from Fiona in the middle of the table.

It read, "The imam will visit 08:00 hours tomorrow. Be awake, articulate, and presentable."

"Shit!"

CHAPTER NINE

Thursday morning, Thursday lunch

The imam was on time.

The minutes leading up to his arrival were a blur of coffee, dressing, and Fiona saying things that Peter only half heard.

Peter opened the door. A pale-skinned Pakistani or Indian man in his early thirties stood outside. He was dressed in a dark business suit with a purple shirt and white tie.

In a broad London accent, the visitor said, "Alright? I'm Hami. Ms. Chapman up yet?"

"Um...yeah, sure. Come in."

"Ta! I haven't got long, yeah?"

Peter was confused.

Fiona called from the kitchen, "Hami! In here. Thanks for coming."

"Ms. Chapman, always a pleasure."

"You've met Peter."

"Oh, Peter..." He shook Peter's hand with a force that shook the last of the sleep from his body.

Peter frowned at Fiona who frowned back.

"What's wrong, Peter?"

"Oh, nothing. You are...the imam?"

Fiona rolled her eyes. "Yes. Hami is in charge of the whole development of the Cultural Center and Mosque. I thought you'd met?"

"No..."

Hami's head spun from Peter to Fiona. "No..."

Fiona held up a hand and said, "Coffee?"

Hami nodded, "Please."

Fiona motioned for Peter to serve it. "Please have a seat. Now, Peter, what's going on?"

"I met a man called Mufarrij. I talked with him through the fence. I'm sorry, I thought he was in charge!"

Hami laughed. "Oh, I get it!"

Fiona looked at Hami and said, "Ah. That means you may not know what's happened."

"I know I've never been invited in here before. And I know you wouldn't be here if something big weren't up."

Peter set the coffees down on the table and sat down before Fiona could send him anywhere else.

As the other two took their seats, Peter launched straight in. "How do you two know each other?"

Hami smiled and said, "We met over dinner. One of the Lord Mayor's banquets, wasn't it?"

Fiona nodded.

"And," Peter continued, "aren't you a bit young to be an imam?"

Hami looked him in the eye and said, "So I was a bit of a swot! Got credentials if you need 'em, yeah?"

Fiona interrupted. "That won't be necessary. Now Peter, who the hell is Mufarrij?"

Hami nodded. "That I can answer. He is one of those lost souls looking for a way. We've taken him under our wing in the hope he won't stray too far."

"A wacko," Fiona said in summary.

Hami nodded again. "Fair enough." He paused and added, "Like Bart."

Fiona said, "You know Bart's dead?"

"Murdered in his bed, I hear."

"No, here in the kitchen."

Peter's hand stopped, his mug at his lips. He saw a stony flash in both their eyes.

Hami held his smile but said, "Do I get the gory details?"

Fiona, matching his smile answered, "If you like. His head was by the door. His body was down here." She indicated where she was sitting.

Hami said nothing, his eyes locked with hers.

Peter couldn't believe what he was seeing. Fiona hated Hami, or at least thoroughly distrusted him. And as far as he could tell, for all the bonhomie, it was mutual.

Fiona continued, "We are thinking some sort of ritual sword."

"Are you?"

"Mufarrij got one?"

"Prob'ly."

Neither of them had moved a muscle. Both intent on each other's faces.

"Detective Mason will want to speak to him."

Hami looked away. He picked up his mug and drank some coffee. "Might not be for the best, yeah?"

"Hami, you know where this is going."

He nodded. "Across the barriers between church and state, what's private and public, what's my religion and what's yours."

Hami locked his eyes on Peter's. "What do you think? You think this is the first beheading of the great new jihad?"

Peter frowned. "I think someone had it in for Bart."

Hami didn't reply or look away.

Nor did Peter. "I don't think it's likely to have a geopolitical dimension. Nor do I think you are someone who goes in for that kind of paranoid rhetoric."

Hami glanced at Fiona and sipped his coffee.

Fiona said, "We have to investigate. We have to do it quietly. We don't want to give anyone reason to create a fuss."

"Fair enough," Hami said, "You've made your point."

A silence followed, in which Peter became more and more uncomfortable. Fiona was still and inscrutable. Hami stared at his coffee.

"Here's what I'll do," he said at length, "I'll announce the police humbly requested our help. I'll have my people have a quiet word with the hotheads. It'll take a day or so."

Fiona said quietly, "Thank you."

Peter said, "The fence moved again."

Hami nodded and said, "Just push it back. It'll be a while before the work starts up again. It's no harm to let 'im play."

Fiona said, coldly, "I disagree. This is no time to have loose cannons on deck. Keep him out of our way...well out of our way."

Hami scowled, but nodded.

Emboldened, Peter asked, "When will the work start again? What's the problem?"

Hami's lips tightened, and he said. "As Ibn al-Mubarak said, 'Perhaps a great deed is belittled by an intention. And perhaps a small deed, by a sincere intention, is made great.'"

"Thank you, Peter," Fiona said, "That will be all."

* * *

Peter wished he could have heard the rest of the conversation.

After the imam had left, Peter stood in the kitchen doorway, watching Fiona.

"I hadn't intended for you to sit with us," she said flatly.

"I know. Tell me about him."

She shrugged. "Harrow boy. Oxford. Did some religious training somewhere sunny. North Africa, I think."

"Sounds more Wealdstone than Harrow."

Fiona laughed. "That's a good one."

Peter shook his head. "He's a used car salesman, not an imam."

"He's a savvy political operator, with family connections. He can be anything he wants to be. Right now, being King of the Building suits him fine." She looked up at Peter. "I'm glad you were there though. I hadn't intended it, but it was useful."

"In what way?"

"He didn't know who you were, or what you are. And you didn't tell him."

"That doesn't seem very useful."

"It put him on the defensive. He thought I'd brought in some big gun."

Peter nodded. "Sounds better."

"Don't get ideas. Hami is an important cog in the machine, and between us, we managed to move him."

"You're welcome."

Fiona sighed and checked her phone. "Now, I'm going out. You're staying in. There will almost certainly be a deputation of Bart's parishioners coming with torches and pitchforks. It'll be you they want to see."

"Oh, that'll be nice. Only 'almost certainly'?"

"Can't say to the minute. My guess was they would have organized themselves sooner. These things are never exact."

Peter sighed and scratched his head. "Sometimes I feel like we're just your puppets!"

Fiona gathered her papers, smiled, and said, "Don't worry, you're very good at it."

* * *

When the parishioners entered unarmed, Peter had to assume the pitchforks were stacked outside.

He showed two men and three women into the sitting room. The settee was new, but the chairs were ragged and stained. With six people, the room seemed crowded. One man took the more imposing chair and sat forward on it. No one introduced themselves.

"Can I offer you tea or coffee?" asked Peter.

"No, no. Thank you. We don't want to be a bother," the man said.

Peter looked at the others, who all shook their heads and said nothing.

Peter sat on a straight-backed chair and said, "How can I help you?"

"Well, let me say, first, we feel terrible about this business." They all nodded.

"You liked Fr. Samuels?" asked Peter innocently.

"Oh, yes! Wonderful priest! We've been so blessed to have him here."

The other man said, "I come an hour each way for his Mass."

"Really?"

The leader went on. "That's not the Sunday morning, you understand. We attend the Saturday evening Mass."

Peter thought for a moment. There was no Saturday Mass listed on the notice board. "Oh! Fr. Samuels did something special for you?"

"Oh, yes!" All three women agreed, smiling.

Peter waited and smiled back.

The leader said, "You know—well, perhaps you don't, being young. You won't remember the Mass like it always used to be."

Peter frowned. "In Latin, you mean?"

He nodded. "That's right. The real Mass, the proper one."

The other man said, "There are quite a lot of us who don't hold with this trite, modern stuff, all that happy-clappy guitar business."

Peter nodded and inwardly rolled his eyes, quite sure of what was coming next.

The leader continued, "We want to make sure that whoever comes next is of the same mind as Fr. Samuels. We hope the bishop understands the situation here."

"Have you told him? Have you ever written to say how much the Saturday Mass means to you?"

The idea seemed to horrify them.

"Oh, no!! We wouldn't have wanted to get Fr. Samuels into no trouble, you see."

Peter said, "But Pope Benedict authorized much wider use of the Latin. Surely..."

The leader interrupted, "Well, it like depends, don't it? The old bishop tried to stop him altogether."

One of the women said, "So did this one. Harassing him, they were."

The leader held up his hand. "Let's not say too much. We don't know the full story." To Peter he said, "Fr. Samuels suffered terrible from all sorts of persecution, you see. We think it was because of his saying of the proper Mass. There are people out there who try and suppress the church, you know. Our faith is under attack! Fr. Samuels did what he could."

There was silence. Peter asked, "Why have you come to me? I'm only here as a temporary housekeeper."

The leader glanced at him but avoided his eyes. "Well, the truth is, we heard you was the bishop's nephew."

"I am. He asked me to step in and keep things ticking over here until the new priest can be appointed."

The other man said, "So you can tell him!"

"Tell him what exactly?"

The leader frowned and said, "To give us a real priest. One who'll say the proper Mass."

Peter didn't reply, hoping to draw him out further.

The man went on. "See...we feel really strongly about this. Now, let me tell you, I make a fair contribution to the collection here. As we all do." Heads nodded round the room. "And the bishop don't want to think he's sure of that money, if he doesn't want to listen to us."

"And," one woman said, "lots of us help keep this place running. If we went elsewhere it would be a sorry state."

"Hmm," said Peter, "I can certainly tell him. But I'm not sure there's much he can do. There's a worldwide shortage of priests as you know. You can't really pick and choose."

"Well, I know there are churches full of us old-timers, I know a lot of the young priests feel the same as what we do. You tell him! We won't have none of this pop stuff!"

Peter sighed and said wearily, "Was there something else?"

"Well," said one of the women, "We've been told nothing about funeral arrangements. We've been told nothing about what actually happened to him. I think there's some sort of cover-up going on."

Peter asked, "Have you been interviewed by the police yet?" Three nodded. "And you've seen the announcement. They think a burglar came in. Until the investigation is done, I don't think they are allowed to hold a funeral."

This seemed to make sense to them all.

As they were leaving Peter said, "It's nice to hear such good things about Fr. Samuels. I had heard he could be a bit difficult sometimes."

"Oh, well...," said the leader, "he was our priest. People respected him for that. He was in charge. That's how it should be. They try and be your best friend nowadays, don't they? It's not right."

After they had left, Peter went to the kitchen and splashed water on his face.

* * *

Ellie appeared from the church.

"Ah, Peter! I'm glad I found you."

"Hi, Ellie. Bit of a busy day today, can't really stop to chat."

She smiled and replied, "I quite understand. I just wanted to say I hope my boys aren't making too much noise."

"Your boys?"

"Well, loosely speaking. My own children are far more disciplined than Doctor Wallace. But, what can you do? You hire the best, even when they lean to the slovenly."

"Wallace?"

"You have met them, haven't you?

"Yes. But what's your connection?"

"I'm funding them, dear boy! And I want to see I'm getting my money's worth."

"Oh, I see...," said Peter, "you are full of surprises, aren't you?"

"Well, given my age, I'll take that as a compliment. I told you Fr. Samuels and I talked much of The Ambulatory. I had just managed to convince him to let us devote some serious time and money on an investigation, the likes of which hasn't been done in many, many years."

"Um...I got the impression...well, no, that wouldn't be fair..."

"Go on." She gave him a sideways look. "Out with it!"

"They don't have a clue what they are doing, do they?"

She didn't smile or look at him. She sat down on a chair, sighed, and said quietly, "No. But that's not the point, really."

"I'm sorry?"

She looked up into his face. "I am amassing as much information as I can from other sources. But, of course, direct observation is the key. Firstly, we must establish the precedent for investigating. Secondly, we explore different types of investigation. Thirdly, when—finally—those in power who might otherwise interfere have become bored with watching, then, we will be able to begin."

Peter sat down opposite her. "You are playing a long game..."

She nodded.

He continued, "With my uncle, perhaps, and...my houseguest?"

"I hope I don't put you in a difficult position."

Peter smiled. "I'm just the temporary caretaker. Soon enough you'll be chatting into the night with a new priest, and I'm sure Ms. Chapman will have more important assignments once the new building is finished and opened."

"I've had practice at patience, Peter. It's something I'm very good at!"

Peter thought the church would do very nicely if it ever did try to sell St. John's, there being two parties with money to spend.

As she left, through the door to the church, she said, "Make sure you get plenty of sleep, young man. The comings and goings here, I'm sure, will not be what you are used to. And don't go wandering in The Ambulatory at night!"

"Um...not on my agenda, thank you."

She nodded. "Good, very good."

Peter thought, *What an odd woman!*

Though, over the next hour, the seed she had planted grew. *Why not at night in particular? It's dark in there in the daytime. What happens at night? What could be worse than the feeling of the expanse opening up in the dark around you?*

* * *

Fred appeared at lunchtime. He brought a powerfully fragrant Indian takeaway.

"Where's mine?" Peter asked.

"It's only round the corner."

Peter handed him a stack of papers. "That's the best I can do with the comings and goings of parish life, with what names Bart had associated with them. I suspect he hasn't updated much in the last few years."

"Great! Thanks. I'll have someone cross reference with what we've already got."

Fiona returned and opened the kitchen window.

Fred began, "Got the pathologist's report."

"Ceremonial sword?" asked Fiona.

Fred shook his head. "Not certain. No definite ID. Described as 'extremely sharp, probably about two foot long, maybe not very wide.' Funny sort of machete?"

"They are usually wide," said Fiona with more confidence than Peter thought proper.

"The wounds and blood pattern are odd too. It looks like he was gored first—plenty enough to kill him. Then his head taken off after."

"Sounds like it would require strength and skill, or utter mad frenzy," said Peter.

Fred nodded. "Not sure what to make of it. Might have been both."

Fiona stood and looked out the kitchen window. "Someone may have had the opportunity to practice this sort of thing. Someone who isn't from around here. This is bad."

Fred said, "It would narrow it down."

Peter thought for a moment. "Not a parishioner, then."

"Nor your uncle," said Fred, smiling.

"He's on your list?"

"He says he was about to sack Bart, farm him off to some hole in the country. I did wonder if it was a case of 'who will rid me of this troublesome priest,' if you know what I mean."

"Ah, Becket...The church tends not to deal with trouble that way anymore."

Fiona said ominously, "In some countries it might."

CHAPTER TEN

Thursday afternoon

Dave called midafternoon.

"We were talking about you earlier," Peter told him.

"Oh, I hate to think...You can put up a notice saying Fr. Matthew Robson, from the Oratory, will be celebrating the Masses on Sunday."

"Righto. Will he need feeding and watering?"

"Might be nice. Anything urgent I should be worrying about?"

"Some scientists are mooching around The Ambulatory and the Tridentinists have been by."

"Oh God! What happened?"

"They're holding their collection money hostage until you replace Bart with someone else who'll do 'The Real Mass' not this Vatican II shit."

Dave was silent for a moment. "Oh, you got off lightly then. Okay."

"They knew we were related."

"If only charity spread as easily as gossip..."

"Anything you want me to do for them, or about them?"

"Oh no. Letting them vent was your good deed for the day. Refer them to me if it gets any more than that. I can send them a brochure on the appropriate circumstances that the Latin is to be celebrated in the Archdiocese."

"Will do. Um, they had their own 'special' Mass on Saturdays. What should I say about it?"

Dave sighed again. "Put up the notice about Sunday. Don't mention anything else."

"Okay. You won't be asking Fr. Robson to do it, then?"

"He can if he wants, but you know...it's not the Latin that I object to, it's the bloody attitude they have about it. Talk to them about Mass as an encounter with Christ whatever the language and they look at you like you've two heads. Well, that's my problem, not yours. Anything else happening?"

"I've given Fred the lowdown on what I could find of parish comings and goings, not that I saw anything relevant. Oh...and the hall is full of Morris dancers the whole weekend."

"Well, you'll enjoy that!"

"I will?"

"If I remember rightly, you have a taste for good beer."

"True. I'm already best buddies with the landlord of The White Hart."

"Well, just don't forget you still have to get up in time to open the doors each morning!"

"Yes, Your Grace..."

"Don't be cheeky!"

CHAPTER ELEVEN

Thursday evening

Peter opened the hall to a couple of nerdy youngsters announcing themselves, the 'Bagman' and the 'Ragman' of The Green Morris, the host for the feast.

Then he posted the notice about Masses on the church door. Inside the quiet of the church he paused to pray, before taking a tour of St. John's formidable statuary.

The occupant of the first alcove beyond the altar was a nun—dressed in what Peter liked to call a burka—kneeling in ecstatic prayer. The dagger protruding from her heart was so realistic it even had a bloodstained handle. In the next alcove was an apostle, Peter thought, though he had no idea of which one. The fire of the Holy Spirit was depicted as a flame descending onto the top of the apostle's saintly head.

He turned to find Ellie standing near the back of the church, watching him.

She smiled. "Peter, I wonder if I might trouble you?"

He waited for her to walk up the aisle.

She said conspiratorially, "I'd like to check up on my boys' progress down below. Would you come with me?"

"Into The Ambulatory? Why?"

"There's also something I'd appreciate your unbiased opinion on."

He shrugged and said, "...Okay. Didn't you say, not to go wandering in there at night?"

"Oh, it's early yet."

She led him down the ancient steps into the circular room. Wallace's gear was in disarray. Cables lay curling along the floor and running back into the dark of the tunnel mouth.

She shook her head and muttered.

"What was it you wanted to show me?" he asked.

She smiled again, nodded toward the tunnel, and walked on.

The cables followed the wall as it curved to the right and snuggled into the join of the wall and floor. Peter's eyes adjusted to the dimming light, still seeing Ellie's white hair before him. His hand stroked the stone of wall along the indented track, worn by so many hands through the ages. At several points, his fingers hit thin upright posts where Wallace had installed equipment above head height.

After a short while, Ellie said, "I want to go slowly as we come to the bend."

As soon as Peter was aware of cold air to his left, Ellie stopped. She turned and said, "Here it begins. Do you feel the air?"

"It's cold," he replied, "and there's no wall opposite us."

She walked on until the curve began to tighten and the darkness was absolute.

"Reach out to me!"

Confused, he checked his right hand was against the wall and reached out with his left.

She grasped hold of his sleeve and slipped her hand into his. Then, letting out a childlike giggle, she swung herself away from the wall. He felt her grip was tight, but instinctively held her tighter.

She whispered, "Where are we, do you think? Do you ever wonder what is out here? So much darkness! Such mystery!"

"Ellie! Be careful!"

Though small and slight, she almost pulled him away from the wall. He shifted his feet to brace himself.

As far as he could tell, she was swaying, perhaps dancing.

"Ellie!"

"What do you think, Peter? Would it be safe to explore?"

"No! Of course not!"

She laughed.

Suddenly she was still.

Her voice was strong in the dark. "So, what do you think? What is this darkness? Are we somewhere or nowhere? Are the entrances we know perhaps merely back doors, and out there..." Her voice faded and returned. "There, perhaps, is the front door, just a few steps into the dark?"

"What are you talking about? Come back to the wall!"

"I'm afraid we're missing something terribly obvious about The Ambulatory just because we are afraid to walk out, to let go of the wall, to find out more!"

Peter began to pull her in toward himself and the wall. She giggled again and slipped her hand from his. He fell onto his backside, up against the wall.

"Ellie!"

There was a long moment of silence before he heard her impish voice. "I'm still here." Her face was close to his.

"Come," she said, "I put more custard tarts in Fr. Samuels' refrigerator for you."

"What were you trying to do?"

"Come on! Feel your way back."

Suddenly unsure of which way was which, he said, "Can we?"

He felt her hands reaching down for his. She placed his hand against the wall and kept her fingers wrapped round his as he got up and they slowly stepped their way back into the twilight of the first curve and then to the circular room.

"You see," said Ellie, as they stood and looked back into the mouth of The Ambulatory, "One can go in and return to this side without trouble. One can step a short way from the wall and not be lost."

Peter clenched his teeth and kept his mouth shut for a moment. He was boiling with fright and anger.

"That," he said quietly, "was a crazy thing to do!"

"Peter! I'm flattered you care so much; we hardly know each other. I was in no danger. I've done it before."

"What I said remains. It's a crazy thing to do."

Ellie turned to him and said, "Ask yourself if you want to know more about this Ambulatory. I'm the only one in a position to investigate it properly. You already appreciate that, I think."

Peter said nothing in reply.

She smiled and winked. "Custard tarts?"

Back in the kitchen, Peter faced Ellie and sighed. "It's late. Perhaps you should be going."

A little disappointed, she replied, "Of course, Peter. Goodnight."

He showed her to the front door.

Alone once more, he called John Marx.

"Sorry to call so late…"

"Not at all, my boy, how can I help? Is there a problem?"

"Ellie was here."

"Ah, bending your ear about The Ambulatory, no doubt."

"Worse than that. She took me down there and…almost went off into the dark."

Marx paused. "Oh dear! She would be embarrassing to lose. Fred would burst a vein at that!"

"Do you…has anyone…measured it, out there—in there?"

"Off the path? Oh, yes. Several attempts. Let me think…Probably the most famous story was a navy captain—Banbury, I think it was—in the seventeen hundreds. Took his crew down with all the ropes and lanterns he could find. Tied them together and told them to walk out in a line and see what they could find."

"And…?"

"They found it was dark, Peter."

"That isn't helpful."

Marx laughed and said, "Welcome to—what would the young people call it?—Ambulatory Frustration Syndrome? It's what we've lived with through the years."

"How many men? How much rope?"

"Ah…your curiosity knows no restraint, does it? I believe the record states something like 'nine cables.' Anyway, somewhere just under a mile. But, sadly, the man at the end of the line didn't come back."

"What?"

"His rope came back but he was no longer attached to it. The fibers had a burnt appearance they said. That's why they didn't do it again. Captain Banbury, though willing to risk his men at sea, felt running experiments underground did not value their lives sufficiently."

"Hmm."

"Don't try it, Peter. Don't let Ellie push you into anything. She's both an adorable little old lady and madder than a herd of cats. Be careful."

Peter muttered, "Understood. Thanks," and was about to hang up when a thought flashed into his mind. "Where is she from?"

"Hmm? Oh, I've no idea where she lives."

"No, I mean, she's not English, is she?"

"Oh, I see...I don't know."

"She made mention of 'your Roman ancestors' rather than 'our,' which I took to mean she's a foreigner...of some stripe."

"Well, I don't know...some of the most famous BBC announcers were foreign, of course. No one born here has quite that impetus for accuracy in speech. Hmm, interesting. I hadn't thought of that. Will you ask her perhaps?"

"No, probably not. I hope it all won't seem so important once I've had some sleep."

"Good night, Peter."

"Good night. Thanks!"

CHAPTER TWELVE

Thursday night, Friday morning

It was after Peter was in bed that the aliens came for him.

The first thing he was aware of was the feeling that someone was in the room with him. He tried to raise his head, but couldn't move.

The voices were strange and quiet, almost soothing. Ellie's voice was whispering orders in a strange language. He could not see her, but as they rolled him off the bed and onto a stretcher, he clearly saw her companions with their large black eyes and oval heads.

Peter saw ceilings go by, then the doorway, and a glimpse of the dirty-looking London sky—and a van. Inside, it smelt like an ambulance, all plastic and disinfectant.

Eventually, the van stopped, and there was a strange rush across a field smelling of wet grass.

Then, he thought, things turned somewhat weird.

He was lifted from the stretcher and forced to run on still-numb legs through a cave or arch onto another field.

Smoke whipped round him driven by a howling gale. The air was uncomfortably warm. It was just as dark as London had been, but looking up, he knew he was in no human city. The buildings were too tall. The waves of smoke left only brief glimpses of endless towering walls pierced by windows lit with many colors. Peter felt dizzy and disorientated.

His abductors drove him on across the field toward a narrowing of the high walls. They burst into a passageway, and he was forced along by a crowd of alien creatures all about four feet tall, all oval-headed, all their deep black eyes glancing up at him as they ran.

Peace—from the running, the wind, the smoke, and the eyes—came when he was guided up a wide staircase into a low building. The house, if such it was, was dramatic in its contrast to the enormity of everything around it.

Through the door, he heard soft music.

Only two of his captors came with him into the house. With his hands held gently in their claws, they led him down a hallway and into a dimly lit room. They sat him down on large cushions and stepped back out of sight.

He was facing a large alien. Not much taller than the others, but obese.

As Peter waited, he saw more in the soft light. He could see the creature's arms were sunk in tanks of gently bubbling liquid. Steam and a sweet scent filled the air.

It spoke, but Peter had no idea what words. He tried to reply but found he again could not move or speak.

The creature lifted its hands from the tanks. Instead of claws Peter could see long fingers. The fingers did not stop but stretched into strands, and the strands into silken threads.

He watched, immobile, as the threads stretched across to him. He felt their softness on his face and the tickle as some explored his ears, and others slipped gently under his eyelids.

Then Peter was not alone, or rather no longer only himself. There was a thought there, a faint inquiry.

Suddenly, as if he were a man drowning, he found his life flashing before his eyes. Childhood memories flickered—the happy, the sad, the embarrassing, the bright, and the lonely. He saw his father, his father's clothes and military gear, camping trips, the day of uncertainty, and then the face of his mother as she told Peter and his brother the catastrophic news. He saw Dave and dinner, The Ambulatory, Ellie.

It was then, with the face of Ellie clearly remembered, that Peter felt truly in the presence of another mind.

There was a thought, perhaps a feeling, a clear indication of distrust—distrust of Ellie. It was an echo of his own feeling, yet more. There was a conspiratorial benevolence in the thought. There was a recognition of a connection, of a fellowship, in that shared distrust.

Peter's eyes opened. Through the strands of silken fingers, he could see the deep black eyes examining him, the oval head nodding over its gorged body.

Peter woke up aching all over and more tired than when he'd gone to bed.

Fiona was in the kitchen with the morning papers and a pile of letters, as he staggered downstairs.

"Morning, Trowbridge! Ready for the Morris feast? Big day for you."

"Ugh."

"You look like you lost the fight with whoever..."

"Yeah. Rough night. Didn't drink enough."

"Oh, well. You won't be seeing much of me today."

"Hmm."

"Oh for God's sake, get some coffee! Monologues are boring."

Coffee in hand, Peter asked her, "What do you know about Ellie?"

Fiona looked wary.

"Um...is that something I shouldn't ask?"

"No, it's alright. No state secrets there. She's wealthy. She's a force to be reckoned with."

"Personally or politically?"

"Yes."

Peter laughed. "Doesn't surprise me."

"She owns one the biggest—one of the first—DNA analysis companies. Never taken it public. She has the ear of some minor royals. And, strangely, liked to spend time with the late Fr. Samuels."

"She's keen on researching The Ambulatory."

"So it seems."

"She's crazy."

"Agreed."

"Last night—Shit! Was I dreaming about her?—she almost moved away from The Ambulatory wall. Deliberately, stepping out into the dark. She was...I don't know...testing limits. Says she's done it before."

Fiona smiled at him. "Peter, if she's a problem, right now she's your problem, not mine. Good luck though."

"Um...thanks."

* * *

There was a flurry of activity outside the hall over lunch, with a group of parishioners distressed at being denied access. Bart's system for the hall, Peter discovered, allowed for double bookings. He did his best to smooth the ruffled feathers. As he sat quietly making a sandwich for his late lunch, the door from the church opened.

He thought, *No wonder Bart had an attitude, there's no peace in this place!*

It was Ellie, again.

"Hi, Ellie," he greeted her with no enthusiasm.

"Peter. I came to apologize. I gave you a fright last night. I hope you'll let me explain myself."

"Um...I'm having lunch."

"So I see. But I've eaten already, thank you. Let me sit and talk, while you eat and listen."

Peter gestured to a chair.

"Now, Peter, I've said I am investigating The Ambulatory. I have assembled a good team, the best to be found. You've only met Wallace and Brad. There are many others. But there are also...vacancies. I wanted to see what kind of man you are. The Ambulatory can reveal a lot about a person. It challenges us. And I wanted to challenge you. I wanted to find out what sort of man you are."

"Why?"

"I've decided I want you on my team. I can use a good man like you."

"What qualifications do you think I have? I'm not a scientist."

"Scientists can be easily purchased, good men less so."

"I'm flattered. But you need skills for an investigation that I doubt I have."

"I already know you'll fit in."

Peter thought and ate.

She continued, "You don't have to decide now. Please consider my offer. You'll be well paid and well cared for."

"I've heard you own a company. Something about DNA, isn't it?"

She raised an eyebrow. "That is true. I'm fortunate to be secure enough to indulge myself in other pursuits."

"I'm wondering what DNA, or running a company, has in common with The Ambulatory."

She smiled. "You have a good mind. I don't want to see you waste it. You know, my husband was a Peter too. You remind me of him."

CHAPTER THIRTEEN

Friday afternoon into Friday evening

Peter was in the church, changing the sanctuary lamp's candle, when a team of dancers arrived through The Ambulatory. About twenty men emerged with overnight bags and bedrolls. Some wore ordinary clothes, some in cricket whites with pewter tankards hooked to their belts. To Peter's surprise, they were of mixed ages, the oldest silver-haired and spritely, the youngest barely of drinking age.

Peter followed them to introduce himself. A coach pulled into the end of the road, its brakes hissing like a geyser. Another phalanx of dancers disembarked. The road echoed with greetings and whistles. As they moved to mingle with the team from The Ambulatory, Peter could hear the occasional jingle of bells.

Two men sought out Peter in the chaos.

"Hello, I'm Mike Dawlish, squire of The Green Morris. We're the host of this feast."

"I'm Roy Majors, squire of Trafford Morris."

"Good to meet you both! Peter Trowbridge, temporary caretaker. You've heard what happened?"

Both men nodded. Mike said, "Never easy when something like this happens. Any word on who might have done it?"

"A random burglar is the latest theory." Peter shrugged.

"So," Roy asked cheerily, "it's you we call when the toilets block up?"

Peter reluctantly nodded. "I suppose so." He thought for a moment. "Do you guys come through The Ambulatory a lot?"

Roy frowned and said, "Not really. Certainly, a lot more of late, what with arranging all this. Why?"

"Just wondering. Did the police get to you all yet?"

He shook his head. "No, I haven't heard them wanting to." He shrugged. "I doubt we'll have much to tell."

Peter left them and went to the toilets to check on the inventory of paper and soap. He kicked himself for not thinking about it sooner.

On his way out of the hall he stopped Mike and asked, "Two questions, if I may? Where are you lot sleeping? And what's a Ragman?"

"Oh, easy ones! We break down the tables later and set up cots in here. The ladies' teams do the same up in the Tap Room above the pub. As for the Ragman, he looks after the kit. Makes sure everyone's gear is up to snuff, you know? Can't be dancing if your baldrics aren't matching! I suppose the kit is as much of the tradition as the dances."

One of the dancers from the bus was standing near and said, "Our Ragman sews up rips and rehangs bells. Sometimes he does it during a dance!"

Mike laughed and said, "Oh, I've seen him! Quite a show."

Peter asked, "And the pewter tankards are part of the kit too?"

They laughed, and Mike said, "Certainly traditional, but really more practical. When we're out touring tomorrow, we won't always have time to dance and finish a pint in one pub before moving on to the next. You don't want to waste it!"

Peter nodded and said, "I can see that."

"Speaking of pints," Mike continued, "You'll be here for a couple later, won't you?"

Peter smiled. "Thanks! I've seen how Jack's been taking care of the barrels."

"Brilliant! See you later!"

* * *

After a couple of pints, they persuaded Peter to stick a note on the rectory door saying "I'm in the hall if you need anything" before he came back for a couple more.

Peter, Mike, and several others sat drinking their beer near the front of the hall. The musicians were at the far end. The center of the room was clear for dancing. Peter watched as dancers gathered in multiple groups of six men, in two lines of three, facing the musicians. After a bar or two of music, they all erupted into motion, handkerchiefs in unison. The striking "chink-chink" of their bells filled the air. Each dancer had four rows of small brass bells strapped around each calf sounding at every movement. The din of five accordions, three concertinas, several fiddles, a couple of drummers, and so many bells was loud even where Peter sat.

"They all seem to know what they're doing!" Peter commented.

Mike shrugged, "That's why we practice."

An older gentleman to Peter's right leaned over and said, "There are two great mysteries of The Morris. Why more people don't do it, and why so many of those who do are so bad at it!"

This drew laughter from the others. He continued, "See yon fellow there, in that set." He pointed to a nearby burly man with a salt-and-pepper beard and a large beer belly, glancing nervously at the other dancers. "He's more on the wrong foot than the right one!"

Mike nodded in agreement, and in the same tone of voice repeated, "That's why we practice."

Peter thought and said, "I was in Nepal a couple of months back and there was a...some sort of festival. I saw a troupe of African dancers doing something just like this. They were all women, in animal heads, but they did the same lines and moving toward each other and circling round. Really similar!"

One of the others said, "Not surprising. No one knows where it all comes from, but 'Morris' might be from 'Moorish,' which would point to Africa."

Two things surprised Peter: how long the dances lasted and how athletic the moves were. He got thirsty just watching.

A young man wearing a white shirt and trousers, and the red and orange ribbons of the Trafford team, came rushing through the front door of the hall. A cheer went up from his teammates.

"Rick!"

"You made it!"

"Here he is!"

Rick already looked red in the face from running. Pausing, he clicked his heels together and bowed theatrically. He was escorted to the kitchen to have his tankard filled.

Peter asked, "What's the story?"

"Girl trouble!" Roy answered. "He's engaged, maybe, to an Indian princess."

Peter looked doubtful.

Another Trafford man said, "That's one rumor—that her family is obscenely wealthy. The other is that they're after Rick's money!"

"I like the Hindu princess theory," Roy added. "He's been through the wringer with her family this past week, though. We weren't sure if he'd be here at all. Oh...," Roy put his hand on Peter's arm, "Careful what you say about Fr. Samuels. Let's just say—Rick—not a big fan."

Peter nodded and determined to find out why not.

* * *

It took a while for Peter to arrange getting a drink at the same time as Rick. He had to break off a conversation with the salt-and-pepper bearded dancer, who was confessing to being "something of a newbie" to it all.

"Hi, you're Rick, right? I'm Peter, temporary caretaker here at St. John's."

"Oh...Hi."

"Were you here on Monday for the practice?"

Rick looked uncomfortable and shook his head. "No, we weren't here Monday. We had a joint practice admin thing Sunday afternoon".

"Oh, right! I was just wondering if you saw much of Fr. Samuels."

Rick scowled and looked around the room. "Yeah. Saw him, alright, on Sunday afternoon, more's the pity."

Peter frowned. "Um, why do you say that?"

"Riya—that's my fiancée—and I saw him...you know, went to talk about getting married. I skipped out of practice for half an hour when she came through. We'd been wondering about doing the wedding here rather than Manchester. She's got more relatives here than there. What a mistake!"

"Oh shit...let me guess. He wasn't encouraging."

Rick snorted, "Bastard! He went on and on about us 'living in sin' before the wedding...and how all our kids would have to be brought up Catholic. Oh...and how he wanted her to give up being Hindu." He shook his head rapidly. "A disaster from start to finish!"

"I can see it all."

"I mean, I know all that stuff, but there are lots of mixed marriages that work out fine. He was...well...it was the way he talked to us, more than anything. Riya was in tears after." Rick laughed humorlessly. "What an idiot I must have looked running up The Ambulatory after her in my full kit, pleading for her to come back..."

"I'm sorry. Are things better now?"

Rick shrugged. "The engagement's been off and on all week. She's talking to me, but the family don't want me around. Won't have their daughter 'talked to that way.' But I'm not staying here tonight—I even changed up there—I'm going straight back up."

"Well, if you find yourself stuck here after hours, just knock on the rectory door, I'll open up for you."

"Okay! Cheers, mate."

Peter watched Rick take his drink and stand with his teammates to watch the dancing. *Oh Bart,* he thought, *was that really necessary?*

* * *

After he had locked the church doors, Peter sat in the kitchen with a freshly made sandwich on a plate and a UFO magazine open on the table.

The door between the kitchen and the church opened.

"Hello?" a voice called.

Peter sighed and held his head. "Who's there?"

"It's me, Sean." The yellow-clad cyclist filled the doorway. "Can I talk to you?"

Peter tried to remember what John Marx had said about not letting Sean into the rectory. *Too late now,* he thought. Aloud, he said, "Um, it's a bit late in the day, Sean."

"Yeah, sorry. But I really need to talk to you. It's about Bart. Is it alright?"

Peter sighed and waved him in. "Hungry?"

"I'd drink some milk if you have it."

Peter went to the fridge and pointed Sean to sit at the table. "Where's your bike?"

Sean nodded back toward the church. "I just lean it up against the front pew when I come in here."

Sean picked up the magazine and asked, "Is this Bart's?"

89

Peter nodded.

Sean said, "He was always going on about aliens. He was going a bit odd, I think. Do you believe in them?"

Peter shook his head. "Never seen anything to convince me. And these mags don't help. They're hilarious."

"Bart did."

"Um...he ever dress up as one?"

Sean snorted. "What? Why would he do that?"

"You do most of your work in Manchester?" asked Peter to change the subject.

Sean nodded, "Yeah, regular clients. Enough to keep me going." He took the glass of milk. "Cheers."

Peter sat and looked at him. Sean avoided eye contact.

"So, what's up? What did you want to say about Bart?" Peter asked.

Sean said quietly, "He was a nice man. He was okay, you know? I know...people didn't like him. But I'm really sad he's gone."

Peter didn't know what to say and so said nothing.

Sean drank the glass in one go. He hung his head a moment and belched. Glancing at Peter, he said, "Look, you do know what I do, right?"

"Deliver packages?"

Sean laughed, "Yeah, sort of...only...I'm the package."

He watched Peter to see if he had understood.

Peter said, "Um, wait..."

Sean continued, "It's a great act. I can go anywhere, anytime, and people assume they know what I'm about. Some of the guys are married and have happy little home lives, probably. I'm a bit of an adventure they can have during the working day, you know? There's one who's in charge of a mailroom. He just closes up for lunch and we have the place to ourselves. He's happy."

Peter took a large bite of his sandwich to avoid saying anything.

Sean shook his head. "I even have to actually deliver letters occasionally, just to keep up the illusion. I charge extra for that." He flashed Peter a smile. "Does that shock you, Mr. Temporary Caretaker?"

Peter swallowed, nodded, and said, "That people still write letters? I suppose it does."

Sean laughed.

Peter asked, "What about Bart?"

Sean nodded and smiled, looking into his empty glass. "It took me a while to suss him out."

"Did you...visit regularly?"

Sean straightened up and lost his smile, taking Peter's question as a challenge. "Yeah. Regular. But, that's just it..."

Peter watched as Sean's face softened.

"I liked him."

"Go on," Peter said, quietly.

"He was the only one who..." He glanced up again. "He never wanted much. He was the gentle sort. But...he wanted me...he wanted me to sing to him. He was the only one who ever did that. It really meant something to him—to have me sing him songs."

Peter got up and put a box of tissues on the table. Sean took two, blew his nose and wiped his eyes.

"No one's ever asked me to do that...only Bart." Sean was quiet for a while. "How did he die?"

"Burglar, they think. It was...probably quite quick." Peter didn't want to say more.

"Upstairs?"

"Here."

Sean frowned. "Okay. It wasn't someone else then?"

"Um...you mean? Oh...no, I doubt it."

Sean was silent for a moment. "Thanks...Thanks for the milk. I should be going."

Peter nodded.

Sean gave him a flash of his eyes and said, "Unless...you're interested?"

Peter shook his head. "Not I."

Sean shrugged and smiled. "Pity."

When Sean had gone, Peter sent a text to his uncle. Then he picked up the box of tissues to find Sean's business card tucked underneath. He left it where it was and went to bed.

CHAPTER FOURTEEN

Saturday morning

Early on Saturday morning, when Peter returned from unlocking the church doors, he found Fiona sitting at the kitchen table. She held up Sean's card, casually between two fingers.

"Had a visitor I see."

"Came in late from On The Green and came through from the church. It's possible, I suppose, that the murderer did the same."

"Quite possible. Be careful of young Sean. He's well-known to Mason and the Manchester lot."

Peter nodded. "I didn't invite him back." He paused and looked at Fiona. "You weren't here last night."

"No, nor tonight. The sound of bells might disturb my beauty sleep."

"Did you make coffee yet?" Peter peered into the jug.

"I was waiting for you. Don't make it too strong this morning."

Peter shook his head and made the coffee exactly as before.

* * *

Dave was at the door before the end of Peter's first mug.

"Got your message. What's happened?"

Peter glanced back to the kitchen where Fiona was engrossed in the papers. "Let's take a walk."

He took his uncle over to the park and found a bench that looked back toward the rectory.

As they sat down, Peter looked around at the park and wondered, "Oh...is this 'The Green'?"

Dave nodded. "All that's left. The church used to be surrounded by trees and grass. Same up north. Both have suffered from the encroachment of brick and concrete. Nothing like this," he nodded toward the building site, "in Manchester yet, thank goodness."

"I had a visitor last night."

"Is everything okay?"

"No, no, I'm fine. But I learned a couple of things about Bart."

"I probably know, but go on."

"Sean Bates. Bike messenger. Uses The Ambulatory every day."

Dave nodded. "I've had reports from concerned parishioners of his bike being around at odd hours, and he was seen coming out of the rectory too early one morning. What with that, the special Masses, his deliberately opaque accounting, and his universal and undisguised disdain for humanity...poor old Bart's eccentricities were finally reaching a threshold that even I couldn't continue to ignore."

"Sean's the only person I've met who really liked Bart. The Tridentinists liked having him as their figurehead, but I get the feeling they would have dropped him soon enough if he'd stopped delivering the Latin for them. That old lady, Ellie, spent time with him, but I think she has her own agenda too. Sean, though, actually found something to like in the man."

Dave sighed. "I think I've said before, some priests cut a lifetime of wriggle room between being celibate and actually being chaste. Bart was one of them, God help him. I was worried for him when the whole abuse crisis hit. His response, you know, was to abolish all use of altar servers, to ban unaccompanied children from church property...to be generally disagreeable with families. He didn't want anyone accusing him of anything. In a way, you have to admire how conscientious he was about keeping this discrete."

"Really? A rent boy in Day-Glo yellow spandex counts as discrete?"

Dave looked Peter in the eye. "You should see some of the arrangements I've had to deal with."

After a moment, they both laughed.

Peter asked, "How much of this do I tell the police?"

Dave sighed again. "Let's assume they know it all already. I'm sure Sean will have had dealings with them, one way or another. No, Peter, I didn't ask you into the middle of this mess to have you try and cover anything up. Tell them what you know. Be yourself."

"Okay...," he shook his head, "just don't want to be bringing scandal on the church."

"Thank you; it's okay. The church is quite adept at doing that all on its own. Was there something else?"

Peter sighed and drew out his wallet. He handed the photograph from Bart's locked draw to his uncle. "What do make of this? I found it with Bart's UFO magazines."

Dave was silent and then said only "Hmm."

Peter said thoughtfully, "I hadn't pegged Bart as the sort to enjoy fancy dress parties."

Dave looked away into the distance. "He talked to another priest once...about demons. He said he thought he'd been visited. I wonder if this is the sort of thing he meant?" He shrugged. "We put it down to paranoia." He handed back the photograph. "Think he was abducted by aliens sometime?" Dave joked. "Might explain some things!"

Peter laughed. "It's not funny! I'm already having bloody nightmares! Anyway, why would they pick someone like him? Actually, my fear, when I first saw it, was that it was a souvenir of some bizarre sexual role-play. While I didn't ask Sean for all the gory details, I got the impression Bart wasn't into anything quite that exotic."

Dave shrugged.

They sat for a while listening to the dancers waking up in the hall, Jack opening windows at the back of the pub, a couple of skinheads holding a loud conversation on the main road. The sound of coaches grew louder. With a raucous chorus of beeping, three of them backed down the street in a line. Two others parked across the end of the road.

Dave said, "Have you checked the bathrooms in the hall recently?"

"No. The last time I was in there, an accordion player was peeing and playing a hornpipe at the same time. Don't make me go back..."

"Humble work is good for the soul. Our Lord worked as a carpenter. St. Paul sewed tents."

"That isn't helping."

Dave smiled broadly and shook his head. "I'll give you ten percent more...danger money."

Peter smiled back. "Deal."

* * *

Dave and Peter mingled with the dancers as they sorted out which teams would ride in which buses. Peter shook his head at the bewildering list of pub names and shopping centers where the dancers were headed.

He asked Mike, "How do you keep it all square?"

Mike laughed, "It's a well-oiled machine! But if someone's on the wrong bus, can you imagine the ragging he'd get from his teammates? The hard work is done—getting the permits and permissions—the rest is a kindergarten assembly."

"With rather large children..."

"Large, hungover children," Mike corrected.

"Good luck!"

"Thanks! There's food and a seat at the table tonight, if you'd like."

Peter nodded. "Thanks, yes. That'll be great. Is that usual...to invite outsiders?"

Mike clapped him on the shoulder and said, "We're just so delighted you're not Bart!"

Into the mêlée came a flushed Detective Mason.

"Peter? What the hell is this? They can't be parking like this!"

"Really? You're not going to do anything about it, are you? I mean...they'll be off soon."

The detective muttered, "Hooligans with handkerchiefs!" He shook his head. "Got a minute?"

Peter nodded and took him toward the rectory. He turned back to wave his uncle over.

Peter made tea, and the three sat around the kitchen table.

Dave asked, "How goes the battle?"

Fred nodded. "A slog. A long slog."

"No suspects at all?" asked Peter.

"Nothing actionable," he sighed. "I've got papers making fantasy photofits of knife-wielding transvestites, while I've got an actual beheading with a machete. I have who-knows-who coming and going next door with religious and cultural differences like flint and tinder, but no history with Bart that we know of." A loud cheer went up outside as the first bus pulled out. "And a load of drunken louts up and down The Ambulatory. Again, this one is a long slog."

Peter asked, "Could it have been a knife? The beskirted knifer of Clifton Street could have come through from Manchester."

Fred shook his head, "Word is that a regular knife couldn't do the job so cleanly. This was one serious weapon."

"Peter?" Dave asked, "Will you be telling the inspector of your visitor?"

Fred looked up, "What's this?"

"Sean Bates," Peter said.

"He came to see you?"

"Um, yeah. Bart was a customer. He wanted...What did he want?" Peter chose his words carefully. "Bart wasn't just one of his regulars. I think he wanted to know if Bart had been seeing someone else, who might then have attacked him. That's partly why I was wondering about...you know...men in skirts."

"Oh?" Fred looked doubtful.

Peter said, "No. I take that back. I think Sean really wanted to find out if there was someone else. That's one thing. Then he was wanting to suggest to me, that it could have been an encounter that went wrong. But he seemed to think if the attack happened in here rather than upstairs..."

"Well, he's not someone I put much stock by," Fred said.

"Actually...," Peter pressed on, "as far as Bart goes, I think there was some genuine connection...for what it's worth."

"Hmm," said Fred, "Heard anything else?"

Peter sipped his tea. "Yeah. There's a Morris man, Rick something-or-other. He and his fiancée had a set-to with Bart on Sunday. Her family's Indian, possibly wealthy."

Fred nodded. "Okay. Anyone else with her? Family members?"

"Don't know."

"Hmm. It is another source for a ceremonial sword."

"And another unfortunate case of Bart being Bart."

There was a tentative knock at the door. All three looked toward the door to the church. The knock came again.

Peter muttered, "Who the hell is it this time?" and went over and opened the door. "Hello?"

"Hello! Sorry to trouble you." The voice was of a polite young man.

"Come in," Peter said, motioning him to the table.

"I'm sorry to interrupt..."

He cut a strange figure in the sunny light of the rectory kitchen. He was about eighteen with a mop of dark hair, unfashionably cut. His expression was of profound confusion as he stood blinking in the light. He wore a long brown overcoat, with dust and soot on the shoulders and arms. He had a brown cardboard box on a string around his neck and a flat cap curled in his hand.

Peter noticed his scuffed shoes and heavy woolen trousers.

"Would you like some tea?" Peter asked.

"Awfully kind...Please," the youngster nodded.

Dave stood and moved a chair for him to sit down.

"I'm Dave!" he said cheerily.

"Hello, I'm...I'm Reggie. Reggie Smith."

"Pleased to meet you, Reggie. This is my nephew, Peter, and this is Fred Mason."

He pulled the string over his head and neatly slipped the box under his chair. He unbuttoned his coat and stuffed his cap into a pocket, then sat down.

Fred was silent, staring at the youth.

While Peter poured more tea, Reggie was glancing round the room, his frown deepening.

"Is Fr. Wilkinson here?" he asked.

"Who?" Fred replied.

Peter and Dave glanced at each other.

"It's just...last time I was here, Fr. Wilkinson..." His eyes darted around the room again. "How did you repair it all so quickly?"

"I'm sorry?" Dave said.

"I...I think I might be a bit lost. I thought I was in St. John's. But it's all just like new in here."

Dave said, "You are in St. John's. St. John's In The Green."

Reggie nodded but said, "That's where I...I should be. Are you a priest?"

Dave put his finger to his lips. "I'm actually a bishop."

Peter put a mug of tea in front of the lad and pushed a storage jar of sugar across the table toward him.

Reggie's eyes lit up. "So much sugar! Blimey, you must know someone!" He glanced around the table with a broad smile before putting three large spoonsfull into his mug.

He gulped a mouthful and swallowed with delight. "Gosh. Thanks! That last one was a really bad one wasn't it?"

"I'm sorry?" said Dave, "What was?"

"The air raid. We could hear it all the way back in the tunnel."

The three were silent as Reggie drank some more.

"Where do you live, Reggie?" Peter asked.

"Norbert Street, just round behind the brewery."

Peter sat up straight. "Oh, wait! Would that be the Western Brewery?" Reggie nodded.

"Excuse me a moment." Peter stood up and went to the door. He caught his uncle's eye and motioned for him to keep talking to Reggie. He said to Fred, "Um...can I have a quick word?"

Fred nodded and stood up. "Yeah...Sure..."

They went into the office and Peter pushed the door almost shut.

"He's a loony!" Fred said, shaking his head.

"He's a loony in genuine nineteen-forties' clothes. I wonder if we can get a look into that box and see his gas mask."

"Why?"

"Because I've a horrible feeling it's new."

"Oh, come on..."

"The kid's a bit simple, right? He's not an actor. He doesn't know what's going on any more than we do. But there he is! He came out of The Ambulatory. That place is—you know—all bets are off! I think he might be what he appears to be. The Ambulatory has done something—I don't know—new? When he walked through that door, the hairs went up on the back of my neck! That doesn't happen often... except when I look into that tunnel!"

"Look, I'll get him home."

"I really think you need to get...maybe a WPC and someone from social services here. I don't think he can go home. That brewery, Western, was wiped out on one of the last air raids. You know, the famous story of people rushing into the burning building to rescue the barrels?" He looked to Fred for some sign of understanding. "Never mind. He's going to want to go back to Norbert Street, and it isn't there. I'll keep him busy while you call social services." Peter reached up and tapped one of the black and white portraits on the wall. "And read that."

The small label on the frame said "Fr. Albert Wilkinson SDS. 1889-1943."

Fred groaned, "You've got to be kidding me!" and took out his phone.

Back in the kitchen, Reggie was laughing with Dave. "I love football too! I wish my brother was here. We used to play a lot."

"Oh, your brother's away?"

Reggie nodded, "Called up. Mum says I won't have to go...," he tapped his temple, "on account of my head."

"Really?" Dave said.

Reggie laughed, "She dropped me when I was a baby! That's what she says."

Peter thought, from the way he laughed a little too much, she was probably right. He sat at the table again. "Um, I wonder...If you don't mind, Reggie, can I see your gas mask?"

Reggie looked surprised and said, "Like an inspection? I told Mr. Willis, the warden, that I never played with it nor nothing. It's still like it should be."

Peter held up his hand and said, "It's okay. I'm sure it's fine. It doesn't do any harm just to check, does it?"

Reggie looked so guilty, Peter almost changed his mind. The boy pulled out the box, and from it produced a pristine gas mask. Peter took it and felt the clean material. He noticed the strong smell of the rubber. The fittings and the buckles on the straps were shining.

"Very good, Mr. Smith, that's in fine order," Peter said with a smile.

Reggie smiled and said, "Thanks! Er, did you say you was Peter?"

Peter nodded, "That's right."

Reggie slid the gas mask back into the box and the box under the chair. "Is there any more tea then, Peter?"

Dave asked, "So where were you last night, Reggie?"

Piling more sugar into his mug, Reggie answered, "Well, it's a bit funny. I was in the shelter with Mrs. Dawlins. But we got separated. I walked in a bit further looking for her. I'm...not sure how long I was... It's a bit..."

"Do you mean The Ambulatory?" asked Dave, "You used it as a shelter."

Reggie nodded, puzzled.

Peter asked, "Do you ever go through to Manchester?"

Reggie shook his head quickly, "Course not! They're getting it just as bad up there."

"Right..."

"Anyway, it's very dark, once you get round the bend, isn't it? I remember smelling the air, how different it was, like the smoke doesn't get that far. I walked over...It's a long way in the dark...I think I must have fallen asleep. I remember I was really hungry when I woke up, but I couldn't see anything. I didn't know what to do, see, I couldn't tell which way I should go..." Reggie shivered and his lip trembled.

"It's okay, Reggie," Peter said, "That must've been very scary."

Reggie nodded. "I called out for Mrs. Dawlins, but there wasn't anyone there. I kept calling, but then I thought, 'You nutter, Reggie, you've gone and fallen asleep and missed the all clear. They've all gone home without you!' So I tried to find my way, but—you know—it's difficult in the dark." Reggie was lost in his memories for a moment.

His face suddenly brightened. "And then I heard the music! So I followed it. It was faint, at first, but then I could hear which direction it was coming from so I just walked toward it. And then I..." Reggie went silent; then his eyes snapped back to their faces. "But the church is all different inside. How did you get the windows replaced? When I went into the shelter, it was all boards and blackouts."

"What was the music like? What kind of music was it?" Peter asked.

"Well, I don't know really. It wasn't like a big band playing. It was more like...waves. That's it! Waves coming and going, but musical. It was lovely. I was so happy to hear it! Have you ever heard it in there?"

Peter shook his head. "What's the date, Reggie?" he asked quietly.

"Well, must be the tenth."

"Of?"

"October."

"And the year?"

Reggie gave him a sideways look. "1940!"

CHAPTER FIFTEEN

Saturday afternoon

Fred returned to the kitchen doorway shaking his head.

Peter mouthed "What the f...?"

He replied mouthing "It's Saturday!"

Reggie looked up and said, "What is it? What's wrong?"

Peter said, "Reggie, we're trying to get someone to come and look after you."

"It's alright; I'll just go home. I've got a key."

Peter sighed and squared up to the table.

Reggie asked, "What is it? What's happened?"

Peter started to say, "I'm not sure how..."

"Is it Mum?"

Peter swallowed hard and said, "Norbert Street's gone. So has the brewery. You'll...," he glanced at Fred, "you'll have to go somewhere else for a while. Just till we sort out what's happened. Don't worry."

Reggie's eyes reddened. "Was my Mum there?"

"We don't know, Reggie," Dave said and put his arm round the young man. Peter stood and whispered to Fred, "Go get something for lunch. Not a curry! Get a whole loaf and a slab of cheese. Pickled onions if you can find them."

Fred whispered back, "We could get him into a hospital."

"Be like transporting him onto the Enterprise! No way. He has to stay here until you can sort out something better."

"There's a teen crisis line I could try, but it's homestay stuff. They wouldn't know what to do."

ED CHARLTON

Peter had a thought. Looking back at Dave he said, "What about the convent?"

Dave looked up and said, "Holy Cross?" Nodding, he continued, "A minute." He stood up and went into the office to make a call.

Fred disappeared, and Reggie sniffled into his handkerchief. Peter sat opposite the youth again and said, "I'm really sorry, Reggie."

"I want to go back. See if I can find any of my stuff."

Peter shook his head and said, "That...wouldn't be safe yet. Do you want something to eat? We don't have much. I could do you a bowl of soup."

"I am hungry, but I think I want the toilet first. Do you mind?"

"Up the stairs. Go ahead."

"Ta."

While he was gone, Dave returned to say, "I've told them they're to get a guest room ready."

Peter nodded. "Thanks. They could keep him from seeing anything too modern too quickly. How are we going to get him there without him freaking out during a tour through London?"

Dave shook his head, "He's only got to look out of a window. I don't think we can stop that happening. If he is what he seems to be, there's no protection we can offer him."

"We have to try. He's lost everything. And he doesn't understand that yet."

Dave looked into the hallway. "Alright there, Reggie?"

"What's this?"

To Peter's horror, Reggie had brought his electric shaver down from the bathroom.

"Um...that's mine. You shouldn't mess about with it."

Reggie looked guilty again. "Sorry. But what is it? I've never seen anything like it before."

Dave's phone rang. Both Peter and Reggie froze in alarm.

"Excuse me!" Dave stepped into the office again, closing the door behind him.

Reggie looked again at the shaver. "What is all this? What was that noise?" A look of panic crossed his face.

Peter anticipated what he would do and caught him by the shoulders as he ran for the door to the church.

"Hold on there, Reggie!"

"Let me go! Let me go!"

Peter swung him round and pushed him back into his chair. "Not so fast. You're not in trouble! You're not in danger! Listen to me... Reggie, listen to me. It's all right. It's all right."

"It's all weird! You're weird! This place is all wrong! Ever since I went in that tunnel...I want to go back and try again. I want it to be like it was!"

Peter shook his head as he took his shaver from Reggie's clutch. "We'll help you, Reggie. Really. Trust us. We'll get you some help."

"You said Mum might be dead. She isn't! You're bloody fibbing!"

Peter shook his head, "I don't know. I don't know for sure. What did your Mum do?"

"She drives an ambulance. That's why she didn't come down the shelter. She was going to report in. Maybe she wasn't anywhere near...?"

The front doorbell rang. Peter looked at Reggie, who looked at the door to the church. The bell rang again, and Dave emerged from the office to answer it.

Peter said, "This is really horrible. I'm so sorry. But, try and keep calm. Be brave."

Reggie fixed a grim smile and shook his head slowly. "I want to see Mrs. Dawlins. She might know what happened."

"Okay...We'll see if we can find what happened to her."

They heard raised voices and the front door slamming.

Dave stood in the doorway smiling. "Sorry about that!"

Peter frowned quizzically.

"Parishioner come to ask about Saturday Mass times." Dave continued, "Now, Reggie, I've got somewhere for you to stay for a night or two, till we can get you sorted out."

Reggie was holding back his tears. He nodded and reached to pick up his gas mask.

Dave put his hand on his shoulder and said, "Not yet. Have some lunch with us first. Sister Ambrose will be along to pick you up."

"You know where the Holy Cross Convent is, Reggie?" Peter asked.

Reggie thought for a moment. "I think so. They have a first aid post there, and you can leave messages for people—people who are missing." His eyes widened. "They might..."

Peter held up his hands and said, "Again, not so fast. They're going to be busy looking after their guests and saying their prayers. But you can ask."

Dave nodded in encouragement. Peter sighed.

Reggie looked up at him and said, "Is that your wife's stuff in the bathroom, all that makeup and stuff?"

"Wife? Oh, no...that's Fiona's...I mean Miss Chapman's...She..."

Dave came to the rescue with, "She works in the parish office."

"Oh, okay."

The doorbell rang again. Dave was shaking his head as he walked down the hallway, but it was Fred with lunch.

Reggie had a considerable appetite.

* * *

Sister Ambrose arrived in a rusty white van with no windows in the back. Peter was delighted.

She was in her sixties or seventies, dressed in a simple long black habit. Her order had once worn elaborate veils but now no longer covered their heads.

"Your Grace." She bowed slightly to Dave.

He said, "Dave, please, just Dave."

"Yes, Your Grace, of course."

Peter couldn't tell if she was joking or not. He said, "Sister, can I take a moment to explain further what's happening?" As he escorted her into the sitting room, he noticed Reggie looking nervously round the kitchen door.

"A young man needs shelter, your uncle told us."

Peter nodded and invited her to sit down. "Have you used The Ambulatory much, Sister?"

She shook her head. "You understand we are a cloistered order; we would have little need of it."

"Need isn't the point. Experience of it might help you understand..." He scratched his head. "You know what it does though?"

"One may walk through to the north somewhere, I hear."

"To Manchester, and it only takes a few minutes."

She looked as if he were telling her a slightly rude joke. "Really?"

"It's weird, it's creepy, and the scientists who study it have no idea how it works."

She said nothing.

"Reggie—the young man we want you to look after—came out of The Ambulatory a couple of hours ago. He had been in there, lost perhaps, but somewhere...Somehow, he was in there for a long time. He says it's 1940."

She gave him the same look again.

"I know it sounds...odd. But I think he is what he says he is. And I think it's going to be traumatic for him when he finds out it's not 1940 anymore."

Sister Ambrose nodded slowly. "I see...I think."

Peter waited for her to catch up with him. "I'd prefer he didn't see much on his way to you and even less once he's there. Your van is great—but put him in the back. The police will arrange social services and, I imagine, perhaps some sort of counseling support for him. Until then..."

Sister Ambrose nodded more confidently. "How strange, that the very thing for which we are so often mocked should suddenly seem so useful."

Peter frowned and waited.

"Keeping the modern world at bay. People say that stepping into our house seems like going back in time. I presume you are hoping that is so in this case."

Peter relaxed a little.

"But, tell me," she continued, "how sure are you that the young man is not a liar? If we take him into our house, we want to be sure we are not putting ourselves in any danger."

Peter nodded. "I don't know what to tell you. He may not be trustworthy. When I look at him, I see a lad who's a little on the simple side. He's been surviving in the middle of events he doesn't comprehend—the war—and, now he walks into our kitchen. Talk to him. Also, I looked at his gas mask. It's brand new, hardly used, if at all."

"Gas mask?"

"Of course. And he'll be asking you about people missing in air raids, including his mother."

Sister Ambrose looked off into the distance. "You know, I think we have a sister who was a novice at about that time. Yes, I will ask about that. Very well. I will see him."

Peter took her into the kitchen and said, "Reggie? This is Sister Ambrose. She has a room for you at Holy Cross."

Reggie looked scared.

"Now, young man," she began, "I understand you've had a difficult time. I certainly don't want to make it any worse for you. You let me know what you need. We can look after you for a short time. You'll need to do as I say once we get to the house. There are several elderly nuns we are looking after, people worse off than you are."

"Y-yes, Sister," Reggie replied, avoiding eye contact with her as she stood over him.

"And there will be some work for you to do while you stay. Is that alright?"

"Yes, Sister," Reggie straightened in his chair and faced her. "I'll do my share."

She smiled and said, "Very good. Come along."

Fred, Dave, and Peter watched from the front of the rectory as Reggie sat in the back of the van.

"Good call," Peter said to his uncle.

"Ambrose is one of the best," Dave replied and to Fred said, "It's only temporary. We're trusting you to fix the rest."

Fred shook his head. "I've put in the calls. I can't do much more."

"More tea?" asked Peter.

Fred said, "Got to go. I might even see the inside of my own house tonight!"

Dave laughed and said, "'A policeman's lot is not a happy one, happy one!'"

"Too right, mate."

Dave turned to Peter and said, "Nor is a bishop's. I must go too. Good luck this afternoon. There will be people, who didn't get the word, turning up for the Latin Mass."

"I hear Manchester's nice this time of year," said Peter.

Dave shook a finger at him. "You're on the payroll. No skiving off."

"Yes, Your Grace."

"In fact, I seem to remember you'll be strapping bells on your legs tonight."

"I didn't agree to that, did I?"

Dave patted his shoulder and said, "Have a good time. You've earned it."

CHAPTER SIXTEEN

Saturday late afternoon

Almost as if she had been waiting for them to go, Fiona let herself into the rectory before Peter had sat down.

"What was that van?"

"Hello, how are you? How's your day going?"

"Sorry, Peter, you know I...don't do much of that. I'm working. I stay focused."

Peter sighed. "Well, since you hate to not know, it was Sister Ambrose from Holy Cross, taking away Reggie Smith, formerly of Norbert Street."

"Where's that?"

"Under the university dorms, I think. Behind where the Western Brewery used to be."

Fiona shook her head. "Not that familiar with the history of the area."

"Thing about Reggie is, last night he took shelter in The Ambulatory to avoid an air raid. And he came out this morning into the kitchen, looking for a priest who's been dead for almost seventy years."

"Don't be funny, Peter."

"If something like that happened to me I'd probably go insane. So, Ms. Chapman, you're not the only one who's been working. We've been working on damage limitation, trying to get Reggie into a safe environment before he has to face the truth that everyone he knew—what is for him, yesterday—is dead and buried." Peter could feel his temper gathering steam. "And you and your not liking when you don't know shit, and you being worried about people dying...Well, your ignorance of The Ambulatory is certainly going to hurt that kid. What the hell is that thing down there that someone can walk into in 1940 and breeze out of, here, today? Who else has come through it? Who else is lost in there? Why hasn't it been sealed up?"

Fiona looked at him without speaking and then said, "Yes."

Peter blinked. "Yes, what?"

"You are articulating exactly how I feel. Those are my fears, my questions."

Peter opened his mouth, but nothing came out.

"And the bugger of it is, we're hearing chatter that something is going to happen tonight."

"What? What sort of something?"

Fiona tilted her head. "Sit down."

Across the kitchen table and the remains of Reggie's lunch, she said, "I have a dilemma, Peter. It's a straightforward, do-I or don't-I decision."

He said nothing.

"There is an extremist group with a bomb. They're going to plant it somewhere around the Islamic Centre tonight."

"Oh..."

"My choice—my decision—is whether to evacuate the area or not."

"You don't know if you can stop them."

She half shook her head. "No, we could sweep them up. It would be bloody. They might detonate to cover their tracks. We don't know where the bomb is exactly, just that it's sophisticated, portable, and powerful. We know where the people are, not the hardware."

"Hmm. So why not evacuate?"

"Several reasons. It would tip them off, and they might try and improvise. Unintelligent people should not be encouraged to improvise; it never works to the good. It would be a publicity coup for them—they threaten and we jump—it puts them in charge. Also, it might not be necessary."

"Why on earth not?"

Fiona sighed. "If you wanted to blow up a building where would you plant the bomb?"

"Um...wherever it would do most damage."

"And in this case? A sprawling complex that's half open in one section, not even half-built in another?"

"I don't know."

"Well, that's a comfort, I suppose. We think they will try and place it underneath."

"Like in the basement?"

Fiona waited.

"Oh shit..." Peter said.

"That's right. We think they are going to place the bomb in The Ambulatory."

Peter was silent.

She continued, "You mentioned my ignorance. Well, there it is. What will happen if it goes off in there? Will the blast take out the church here? The one in Manchester? Will we even notice? If we can't find that tunnel when we try and map it, will an explosion find us while we stand on top of it?"

"So what will you do?"

"I've already done everything I can. Unfortunately, events are moving faster than I anticipated. I had hoped for a week or two more. If those two boffins could get a consistent video feed from in there, we might have a chance to intervene, if and when the bomb is planted. Without that, I'm at a loss. Without information how do I decide?"

"I wouldn't want your job."

"No. Not many do. The best of all outcomes is that the bomb goes off, nothing gets damaged, and no one ever finds out what happened. They will have shown their hand, failed, and we can then hide them away in one of our nonexistent facilities."

"And the worst?"

"It goes off, destroys all or part of the Centre, people nearby get killed—you, for instance, and perhaps a hall full of Morris dancers. Add to that any other unknowable consequences of a detonation within The Ambulatory, and all in all, it could quickly spiral into a god-awful mess."

After a long silence, Peter said, "You don't believe in God, do you?"

"I have seen little that would give me reason to."

"But you believe in The Ambulatory. You've seen it, heard about it, received reports about it."

"It exists."

"I believe in God...Even if you discount personal experiences, belief is largely about trusting what other people tell you. I've heard about God—received reports, if you like. I look at it like this: if God is who people I trust tell me He is, then He's worthy of my trust too. That's the chain that connects us back to the early church." Peter leaned in over the table. "Your problem is the bit where you have to believe what other people tell you. You don't want to make a decision based on their beliefs." Peter smiled. "You don't trust what anyone says."

"How is this relevant?"

"Oh, never mind. As to The Ambulatory...From what I've seen, less time is taken in transit than should be. You'd expect an explosion down there to travel further and faster. But there's the path it takes; explosions don't like to go round corners. It's well constructed, looks like it's cut out of solid rock, like a bunker. But then there's Reggie. Instead of traveling further and faster, he didn't travel far, and it took rather a long time."

Fiona said nothing.

Peter continued, "So, I'd say it depends where they put it. If they wander off the path...they might not come back at all."

"Did Wallace tell you what happens to electronics?"

"He might have mentioned something." Peter shook his head. "Don't remember."

"It's possible an electronic timer will fail to function, and we'll be able to go in and retrieve it."

"If you can find it."

"He has partial camera coverage."

They were silent for a moment. Peter looked her in the eye. "Oh... Damn you...you've already made this decision, haven't you!"

To his surprise, she frowned. She looked away briefly. "Of course. But I wanted to hear your opinion."

"Fuck you!"

"Really, Peter..."

"I'm sorry. Fuck you...Ms. Chapman!"

She smiled. "You know, my job isn't what you think. It's only partly about the data and information; it really is about the people— who they are—not so much what they believe or say. And...you...you are actually rather good at seeing people for who they are."

Peter was puzzled.

She continued, "I don't know about The Ambulatory, you're right. I can't know about it. I'm knee-deep in inconclusive reports and speculation. But, you are also right. I have already decided. You could see that, and I couldn't. I'm getting in my own way on this and overthinking it. Thank you."

"I'm...not sure I understand..."

Fiona nodded, "That's okay."

Peter shook his head and said, "God, you're annoying!"

Fiona smiled. "Do you know you said that out loud?"

"Someone had to."

Fiona smiled again and said, "Continue with the feast. I have someone there who will protect you if necessary...if possible. We will also have other...assets nearby."

"You have Morris dancers who work for you?"

"You don't need to know that."

"And the bomb?"

"Comfort yourself with the thought that if you're blown up, you won't have to watch me look for a new job."

"Oh...thanks."

CHAPTER SEVENTEEN

Saturday afternoon into evening

Peter spent part of the afternoon mopping the floors and cleaning the bathrooms in the hall. It wasn't as unpleasant as he expected and gave him a few minutes of solitude.

The Ambulatory loomed large in his thoughts along with the image of Reggie Smith wandering in the dark.

How big is it? From the inside, there's no way to tell. It feels so enormous.

Peter thought back to the drunken boffin wanting to search from the outside.

Reggie must have been terrified.

So must anyone else who wandered in.

Peter had a picture in his mind of the expanse as a dark abscess sitting behind the flesh of English history, always there, always hidden. He breathed in the disinfectant fumes from his mop and turned his mind back to the more practical thought: *Who—or what else—is in there?*

By the time the coaches arrived back, and exuberant dancers once more filled the street, the hall, the park, and parts of The White Hart, Peter had decided to run some ideas by Fred. His own answers to those questions needed the cold water of the detective's common sense.

Peter met Jack in the kitchen of the hall. "How's it going?"

Jack nodded and said, "Yeah, so far so good. Breakfast went okay. I've got good kids working this weekend. Nothing got too cold coming over from our kitchen. Tonight's more of a problem. I need the ovens on here, and they've not been drawing from the barrels in the right order. I daren't risk stirring up the beer by moving them, but the heat will do nasty things to them."

"I get the feeling this lot can make short work of any particular barrel you ask them to really concentrate on."

Jack laughed and said, "True enough. I'll end up being here more than behind the bar tonight I think. Are you staying?"

Peter realized, as he said yes, how much faith he was putting in Fiona, and how much he wanted to warn all these people of their danger.

* * *

The tables were set up around the edges of the hall, leaving room for dancers, musicians, and singers in the center. The top table, of captains and squires from each team, was furthest from the door. Peter sat opposite near the vestibule, his back to the door and the traffic to and from the kitchen passing his right shoulder. He had wanted to call Fred, but the activity, noise, and beer made him put it off.

Harry, the bearded dancer with two left feet, was his neighbor. As they chatted, the man twitched several times, his phone vibrating with yet another message.

"Sorry about this! It's the boss. She hardly leaves me alone."

Peter smiled. "She let you get away for the weekend."

Harry nodded. "True. Physically. I suppose it's something."

A dancer stood in the center of the floor with two musicians. His call of "This one's for Rick!" was met with general applause. They sang:

"When I was single, Oh then, Oh then,

When I was single, Oh then,

When I was single, my pockets did jingle,

I wish I was single again, again.

Oh I wish I was single again..."

Peter shook his head and said, "That's cruel!"

Harry laughed and said, "Oh, not married then?"

After the song, one of the visiting teams performed, to Peter's surprise, a dance with wooden sticks the size of baseball bats, instead of the customary handkerchiefs.

Harry leaned toward Peter and said, "They usually announce this as the most dangerous dance in the world. See that fellow over there?" He pointed to a dancer at another table, eating with one hand, his other in a bandage. "He did this dance at one of the pubs earlier. Blood everywhere!"

The dance was similar to those Peter had seen before, the dancers in two rows mirroring each other, stepping forward and back, round each other, and with great vigor clashing their sticks. The margin for error, Peter could see, was tiny as the dancers struck in time with the music while moving through figures of the dance. In the final chorus— to complement the steps, the strikes, and the turns—they delivered a hilarious, bawdy verse in a rap style. From the catcalls and cheers— and, from somewhere by the beer, a cry of "Flash buggers!"—Peter understood the assembly felt they were showing off a little.

During another team's display dance, Harry was glancing at his phone. He laughed and said, "Whoa! Look who this is!"

Peter, still watching the dance, said, "What's that?"

Harry read: "*The One Daily.* 'How the Mighty Are Fallen.' That's the headline. 'The son of an Iraq War veteran, this once academically gifted citizen was his uncle's bright-eyed boy. Now he works cleaning toilets in a run-down inner-city church. We asked former girlfriend Rebecca Trent, what caused Mr. Peter Trowbridge, 25, to fall so far off the rails.'"

Peter turned to Harry wide-eyed.

Harry read on: "'I always thought he was destined for great things,' said the stunning Miss Trent, 'but then so did he. Better things than me obviously.'"

"That bastard!" said Peter, under his breath.

Harry smiled and looked up. "Pissed someone off, did you? It goes on...'Now it seems, Unlucky-in-love Trowbridge has to rely on the nepotism of the local Catholic church, getting the job through the personal intervention of none other than the auxiliary bishop of Southwark himself. Bishop Davidson, it will be remembered was promoted to the post despite protests over his communistic leanings from ordinary Catholics across the city. It seems that Comrade Davidson has put his underachieving nephew under his protection and compensated him for his inability to find gainful employment with a cushy job in a quiet backwater parish.'"

"Please...stop," Peter said.

"No, that's it. Apart from the picture of the stunning Miss Trent."

"Really?"

Harry held up his phone.

Peter nodded. "Yeah, that's her first professional head shot. I was there when she had it done. How did Treverton find her?"

Harry shook his head. "It's not hard nowadays. Don't worry about it. It doesn't actually say much at all."

"I want to throw up."

"Ha! I feel that way every time I read Treverton's stuff."

"How...How can anyone defend themselves against this sort of shit?"

"By ignoring it, Peter. Keeping calm and carrying on, you know?"

"Easy to say." Peter reached for Harry's phone and then said, "No. I don't want to read it."

Harry stood and patted Peter on the shoulder. "I'll get you another beer."

"Good idea."

As dessert was served, Peter was distracted from fantasies of Treverton's varied and painful deaths, by people gathering behind him in the vestibule. He looked around to see a young Indian woman and two others, perhaps her parents. The man was in a designer suit, impeccably turned out, the woman, in a sari, sparkling with gold.

Harry muttered something Peter didn't catch and was once again absorbed by his phone.

Rick stepped up to the trio in the vestibule and gave the young woman a kiss. He shook the man's hand and nodded to the woman. He turned and with a few jingling steps, took up position in the center of the floor.

At the top table, Mike knocked a gavel. "Gentlemen! And ladies! Rick Dunlop will now dance for us The Princess Royal, a solo Morris jig from the village of Fieldtown in Oxfordshire."

Rick, accompanied by a lone concertina player, performed a dance of steps, turns, and agile leaps, in a controlled flurry of handkerchiefs underpinned by the rhythmic chink of his bells. The assembly watched in complete and respectful silence. The eruption of applause at the end of Rick's dance seemed deafening to Peter.

Peter stood and gestured to let the mother sit down, which she refused wordlessly. To the father he said, "Have you seen this before?"

The man shook his head slowly. "No. Rick has talked about it. But I have never seen this done. They applaud so much!"

Peter nodded, "Earlier they were making jokes at his expense, and now look!"

"Often British people hide their affection behind humor, isn't it?" There was a glint in the man's eyes that Peter instantly warmed to. "Well said."

Rick made his way over, looking flushed and with a broad smile on his face.

Harry stood at Peter's shoulder and spoke directly into his ear. "We must leave."

Peter leaned back away from him and said, "What?"

Harry pointed discretely at Rick's future in-laws and said, "Ms. Chapman says they are going back to Manchester immediately. Move!"

"Shit! Alright—Fiona Chapman—you meant 'boss' literally."

Harry nodded grimly.

Rick said, "Hey, what's going on?"

Harry pushed in front of the older couple, pulled out some form of ID and said, "Mr. Kasthurirangan we believe you may be in some danger if you remain here. I will accompany you and your family back through The Ambulatory, but we must do so immediately!"

Peter said to Rick and Riya, "Um...there's a problem. Can we all talk outside?"

"What sort of problem...?" Rick began.

Peter put his finger to his lips and then pointed to the door. Rick's frown lifted as his fiancée took his hands and led him out.

Peter reached back to grab his sweatshirt from the back of his chair. He was going to ask Harry if he wanted his tankard from the table, but he was already through the door.

As the six of them stood in front of the hall, Riya's father started to say "What is this danger?" but from the main road came the sound of smashing glass, an alarm, and cheering.

They all looked toward The White Hart and could see smoke, backlit in red, rising beyond the pub's roof.

"Let's go!" Harry ordered, "Or we won't be ahead of the action."

Peter led them to the side door of the church and held it open while they filed in. He could see, as he glanced back toward the street, the silhouettes of running figures and hear more shouts, more cheering, more glass shattering.

He closed and locked the door with a sigh of relief. The dark of the church felt warm around him. He reached up to feel for the light switch by the door. It took a moment until he found the button of a rotating timer-switch. The only light that came on was a small bulb above the door; the switch began rattling toward switching off again.

They moved carefully to the front of the pews and toward The Ambulatory door.

Peter looked round the church and was surprised by one of the statues caught by an angle of light from the door: the robed apostle, standing in constant silence in an alcove, with the flame sculpted rising from, or rather descending onto, the top of his head. Peter remembered two things in an instant. The statue was of St. Jude the Apostle who, lacking other signature detail in scripture, is depicted simply as a recipient of the Holy Spirit at Pentecost, symbolized by the descending flame. The shadow of shoulders, head, and flame in the uncertain light were what Peter had taken for a foil hat in Bart's picture.

That picture with the alien was taken here in the church!

Peter felt electricity run through him. Did Bart's photograph show a real alien? Was the nightmare he remembered so vividly more than a dream?

Harry led the party down the steps to the circular room. Peter was last and couldn't see what happened at the bottom. He heard a bang that echoed up the staircase.

He heard Riya and her mother both cry out. By the time he tumbled out into the room, it was all over.

Harry lay on his back, his eyes and mouth open, a large bloodstain expanding through his white shirt.

A scruffy middle-aged man in a short black coat was standing in the center of the room, pointing a gun at Peter. Four other men, younger and similarly anonymously dressed, were pushing Rick and the Kasthurirangans to Peter's left, up against Wallace's tubs.

Footsteps sounded on the stairs and a skinhead, tattooed arms on display, pushed past Peter and said, "Door's unlocked again."

The man with the gun nodded and pointed at Peter. "He'll do."

Peter saw a large metal briefcase on the floor just at The Ambulatory's entrance. As he looked the man in the eye, his heart sank.

Peter had met evil people before. They weren't the sort to cavort with the devil or lay waste to continents; they were dull, mean, and petty. They were people who would offer to write the minutes of a meeting and record what they wanted rather than what happened; to speak when it was hurtful and say nothing when words might help; people who could chill the warmth of their fellows and sour any ordinary activity.

This man was different. This was one of the walking dead. His eyes showed no life. If he felt fear, it was only that someone might stop him doing what he had decided upon. His face showed purpose devoid of emotion. Peter felt the fellow wasn't acting out of devotion or belief, but from a decision, perhaps the toss of a coin, perhaps from a purely intellectual resentment. There was no hate and no love in those eyes.

"This isn't going to have the effect you want it to," Peter said.

He snorted in mild derision and said to the others, "Get the tape."

While one of them brought a roll of insulating tape, another picked up the briefcase.

"Take this." He handed the gun over in exchange for the case. "Shoot him if he twitches." He bent down and plugged a small device on the end of a cable into a hole at the top of the case. To Peter he said, "Hold this."

Peter took the device, and a large hand came from behind him pushing his thumb down on a button. He couldn't resist. In a well-choreographed set of moves, they taped the case to his chest. Peter staggered slightly under the awkward weight.

"Well, you got a choice, mate. Let go of that switch and blow us and them up now...," he nodded to the Kasthurirangans, "or you can wait until you're on your own."

"You bastard!"

"Let's do it!"

They held Peter back while the others were escorted into The Ambulatory.

The smell of old damp stone wrapped itself around them as they stepped into the gloom. The thug on Peter's right placed one hand on the wall, his other hand still firmly holding Peter's arm. His colleague had both hands on Peter's left arm.

The wall curved to the right and the light from the circular room faded. All sounds diminished except for Rick's Morris bells which seemed to be casting an echo.

A voice, seemingly a long way ahead, called back, "We're here! It's the curve!" Peter was aware again of the breeze coming from his left where the dark wall of the other side of the tunnel opened to the huge expanse.

All at once behind him he heard an electronic bleeping, something clicked within the case strapped to his chest, he felt a brief vibration through his ribs, and the hands on his arms swung him hard away from the wall.

"Off you go!"

His head swam, and he fell through the darkness, slithering down the smooth stone slope. He desperately tried to hold his thumb against the button. His elbows and head hit the hard rock several times. He could feel the edge of the briefcase digging into his arms, ribs, and stomach.

Then he lay still.

"Shit!" he blurted into the darkness.

Though he could see nothing, he could still hear something. It was a high-pitched ringing, the echo of Rick's bells folding back from the stone, echoing and reechoing, not seeming to fade, blending into a haunting musical chord.

From a great distance he heard shouts, swearing, then fainter, so faint, a lost voice called and was gone.

CHAPTER EIGHTEEN

Saturday night

The Kasthurirangans rushed out of The Ambulatory, into the circular room of St. John's On The Green, as fast as the mother's sari would allow.

They met with a line of helmeted riot police, each with an assault rifle pointed directly toward them.

"Don't shoot!" Rick shouted.

"Armed police! On the ground! There!" one officer shouted in reply, pointing to the floor to their right.

Behind them, at high speed, came the leader of the bombers. He skidded to a halt, swore and turned to run back into the tunnel.

Someone shouted, "Take him!"

A single shot rang out. He cried out and fell.

Riya's mother screamed.

Two more men jogged out of The Ambulatory. They glanced at the guns and their leader prostrate on the ground. They stood still and raised their arms.

"Where are the others?" the officer shouted at them. The men frowned and looked at each other in surprise.

Still half crouching to one side, Rick said, "We pushed them away... into the...away from the wall."

Four policemen dragged the bomber past Rick, his groans revealing he was not yet dead.

The officer squatted in front of Rick and said loudly and steadily, "Where is the bomb?"

Rick shook his head. "They strapped it on the caretaker. He was behind us. I think they pushed him away like...straight away...still near the other end."

Standing up the policeman ordered, "Get these people out of here!" Blue team here. Green team with me. Hands on the wall!"

With a rumble of echoing boots, half of them jogged into the tunnel.

A small crowd of civilians was gathered at the top of the stairs as the family emerged. One said, "I am John Marx, vicar here. Come with me, please. You're safe now."

He took them into the rectory, through to the sitting room.

"Is anyone hurt?" he asked, "There are ambulances, if there is a need."

Mr. Kasthurirangan helped his wife sit down on the couch. "Are you alright, Mother?"

"Don't worry about me. What about that young man?"

John looked toward Rick and Riya.

"We're okay," Riya replied, "Just pushed about a bit."

"They strapped a bomb onto that caretaker bloke," Rick said.

"Peter?"

Rick nodded, "That his name? Yeah."

John swallowed and said, "You'll need to tell the police everything you saw, everything they said. In the meantime, can I get you anything? Tea?"

Mr. Kasthurirangan nodded, "You are most kind."

* * *

Fiona watched the street from her vantage point in the attic of The White Hart. She could see one of the police lines at the end of the block, the fire at the Tandoori Palace, the twenty or so skinheads whistling and jeering. She couldn't see the church. The smoke from the fire was pouring down the road toward the hall and the mosque site. She knew she would have to move.

She sent yet another text to Harry White. She sent a text to Mason, who replied, "Stay there."

"I need data," she said to the phone. She decided not to reply.

She slid out of the back door of the pub and across the top of the park. The smoke was whipping round the buildings and lifting and falling unpredictably. She covered her mouth and set off toward the side door of the church.

She was instantly enveloped in choking smoke and the nauseating smell of burning plastic. She coughed and swore.

"Who's there?" said a voice.

Fiona stopped. She couldn't see how far she was from the church, nor who had called out. She stepped forward, hoping for a clear stretch of air.

"Whoa!"

A young man had been sitting, his back against the church wall, his head lower than the smoke. He launched himself up and grabbed Fiona by the throat.

"Hello!"

The smoke billowed away, and she saw his tattooed arms and shaven head.

"Gh-ah!" she choked.

He winked at her. "Nice night for a walk, sweetheart."

He pushed her up against the wall. To her right, she heard a rhythmic clacking. He heard it too.

"What the fuck's that?"

"Gh-uh!" she gasped.

Clack, clack, clack. Then she heard bells.

He was distracted enough to give her room to knee him in the groin.

"Oof!"

His hand slipped from her throat to her shoulder. She turned her other shoulder into his chest and pushed away from the wall. He fell, and she fell on top of him. Rolling away she found herself at the feet of several Morris dancers.

To their surprised stares she barked, "Don't just stand there! Help me!"

Her attacker was on his feet, confused. "You fuckers are in for it now!" he shouted.

One of the dancers bounced his stick off the ground and swung it against the shaven head.

Fiona stood over her attacker's prostrate body and said, "Yes, lovely night."

"Are you alright, Miss?" said one of the dancers.

"Fine. You should take shelter in the hall."

"Some of our friends came out here. Didn't want anything happening to them."

"Well, I certainly appreciate it. But I think it would be best if you stayed on guard at the hall doors. Don't let anyone in."

Another said, "We're not leaving you out here on your own, Miss."

"I'm going in the church. Where's Harry White?"

"Harry? He's with the others we're looking for."

Fiona sighed, looking up and down the road. The smoke descended again.

Coughing, she said, "Alright! Into the church!"

* * *

Fred Mason was itching under his riot gear. He hated the heat and the weight of it. He looked again at his phone waiting for a reply from Ms. Chapman. He swore. Then he swore some more. "She's not going to listen, is she?"

He turned to his team in the van and said, "We've got to go into the rectory. In through the back door, out the front and try and escort someone either to the church or the hall. I don't know which."

"Sir? Who's wandering around in this?"

"No one. If we find her, you haven't seen her."

"Yes, sir."

Fred nodded in unspoken agreement that it was a dumb idea.

They moved the van into the end of the alley that ran up to the back of the rectory. Moving at a slow jog until they reached the rectory gate, they stopped and listened before pushing through the gate and bins to reach the door.

Fred elbowed the glass above the lock, reached in and unhooked the chain. There was no key in the lock. He stepped back and let one of the others kick the lock until the door flew open.

To the youngest of the team, he said, "Guard that door inside. If you hear anyone coming in from the church, click twice." He indicated his helmet radio.

He led the others through the kitchen to the front door. All was dark. The smell of smoke was faint.

He opened the door and squatted down and peered up and down the street. He saw a flash of white and of colored ribbon disappear into the church.

"What the...?"

He stepped back into the dark of the hallway. "Back. And into the church."

His team stepped nervously through the doors into the vestry and then out into the main church. The lights were off, only the sanctuary lamp glowed.

He could hear a slight chink-chink sound from by The Ambulatory door.

"Light!" he whispered. Three torches came on.

Across the church were six startled men in whites. In the middle of them was Fiona, her arms crossed, her head crooked sideways. "What kept you?"

Fred smiled. To his team he said, "Guard the doors. Make sure no one's hiding in here. Check behind every statue." To Fiona he said, "Is it already in there?" He nodded toward the staircase.

Fiona said, "Looks like it. I just don't know when. We've sealed up the other end. These gentlemen tell me a party from the feast may already be in here. I don't know what we'll find."

"I can't let you go down," he replied, "nor the civilians."

"I'll call them in," she replied.

She took out her phone, dialed, and without waiting for the other person to speak said, "Come through."

A voice came from the head of the stairs. "Ma'am?"

"That's impressive," said Fiona coolly.

"I'm afraid there's one man down, Ma'am, and one unaccounted for."

Fiona tilted her head instructing Fred to follow her down.

As they made their way down the stairs, she said, "Detective Mason, Sergeant Willis."

Willis said, "Sir."

Fred nodded, "Sergeant."

Fred was surprised to hear Fiona gasp as she saw the body.

One of Willis' team was closing Harry White's eyelids.

Regaining her composure, Fiona asked, "Who's missing?"

"Peter Trowbridge, Ma'am. We have a report he has the device strapped to him."

Fiona stared at him. There was silence for a moment. Fred felt no amount of riot gear or Kevlar would shield them from the look on her face.

She said only, "I don't want anyone wandering around in there.

We will have an organized search." She turned toward The Ambulatory and thought for a moment. "Are the targets all accounted for?"

"No Ma'am. We only have three. There are three more."

"Lock it up. No one goes in until we look at the video."

Fred quietly said, "If Peter's in there with the bomb..."

Fiona glared at him. "If it's gone off, there's nothing we can do for him. Or...it won't go off, in which case he's safe and can wait for us to find him. My concern—our concern—has to be if it is yet to go off." She shook her head. "If Peter's in there with the bomb, he won't come anywhere near either entrance until he's sure it's safe. No one goes in. Not yet."

"Ma'am," Willis acknowledged. Fred nodded, reluctantly. Willis flicked a switch on his helmet and said, "John! No one goes in the tunnel until further notice."

Fiona stood facing the dark opening.

Fred stood next to her and listened. He could hear nothing but more glass smashing out in the street.

"Well," said Fiona, "time to stop Rent-a-Mob having any more fun. We know where the device is, for better or worse."

Fred said, "Right, we'll mop them up."

"Fred? Don't be gentle."

CHAPTER NINETEEN

Later Saturday night

Peter wasn't sure if he had passed out. There was no light, no smell, no sound. The stone under his back seemed neither cold nor warm, just solid and smooth.

He could feel pain from various outlying parts of his body. But his thumb was complaining the worst.

He thought for a while why that might be. Then he remembered the button. He was still holding it down.

"Oh, God...Now what?"

His mind wandered for a while. He wondered what Treverton had said to Rebecca and what she thought he was going to write. He was sure there would be a funny side to it, but at the same time he couldn't see it.

He wondered where he was in relation to the outside world. Fiona had said The Ambulatory did not appear to exist where it ought to be. He thought again what the brandy-sipping scientist had said at The White Hart: time and space being compressed—or was it stretched?—and two strings making a path around a black hole.

He wondered how Fiona would try to retrieve the device still pressing on his chest.

"Like the whole Ambulatory, I won't be where I seem to be, will I? Oh, shit..."

He lay thinking for a long time, going over his conversations with Fiona, with Wallace, with Fred. He thought of his mother, her brother, and his own brother. He went through every detail he could remember of Reggie's account of the dark and how he had heard noises.

Peter had heard scientists talking about the possibility of life on other planets, saying that if life is in one place, it is statistically more likely to exist elsewhere, perhaps abundantly. The chances of there being only one of something—of something being truly unique— are small. In a similar vein, the chances of finding oneself in the interesting bits near the beginning or the end of something are far smaller than those of being in the ordinary bulk of its time.

At the time he heard that, Peter had been reading a passage in the gospels where Jesus talked about other "flocks" he had to minister to. It probably was a reference to non-Jewish peoples, but it made Peter smile to think of Jesus doing a tour of habitable planets, and that ours was just one of many stops he had to make.

But, Peter thought somewhat uncomfortably, that meant Reggie probably wasn't the only one. He might have been the only one to come out of the dark while there were folk in the rectory having lunch. Who else might have walked out? From when?

Peter had a brief vision of Bart being attacked by a clanking medieval knight and then by a bayonet-wielding soldier from World War One.

I should have called Fred...

With his free hand he gently worked his phone out of his pocket. It turned on but showed a weak signal.

He began a text message to Fred: "Worked it out. Reggie is the key. He was #2 and okay. #1 wasn't"

Peter stopped.

The screen faded. He was torn for a second between writing on or pressing "send." As he pressed "send," the phone went black.

Well, if I can work it out, so can you, Fred. You'll get there in the end.

It was silent. It was endlessly silent. He could hear his heart beating, the blood in his ears, the occasional creak of a joint as he shifted carefully against the stone floor.

He wondered how long he could keep his thumb in place.

I'll fall asleep eventually. Best result is to not take anyone with me.

As he lay on his back, he thought long about his father.

Did you come to the same conclusion? Did you think you'd do someone harm?

Best result is to not take anyone with me. He could hear it in his father's voice.

Peter had never imagined anything of the sort before. He mentally kicked himself for never allowing for the possibility that his father had killed himself out of a sense of care for others.

But you were wrong! We were there to help. I am truly on my own. You weren't.

"You were wrong!" Peter shouted out.

Peter dried some tears with his free hand and tried to think calmly through his situation.

He knew the church's view of suicide. And he understood that too often the church's teaching was a minimalist statement in black and white: clarity and simplicity winning out over compassion. He smiled remembering Fr. Finnegan referring to his "colleagues who long for days when priests were shepherds to the simple faithful" and then describing "the simple faithful" as "extinct as unicorns."

Moral decisions, Peter knew, were seldom taken in circumstances of either clarity or simplicity.

He knew the bombers wanted the device to explode as close to the Islamic Centre as possible, a wild hope given the peculiarities of The Ambulatory and one he could thwart now by moving as far away as possible.

He knew that Fiona and Fred would risk rescuers lives to try and trace him, another wild hope here in the dark of the expanse.

He knew he didn't want to die, but was going to as soon as he fell asleep and his hand relaxed.

The moral choice seemed to be to move away—into the expanse—and let the bomb go off.

But thinking clearly didn't really help.

No, Peter didn't want to die. It was not only a feeling of fear but one also of regret and uncertainty. He knew he'd meet his maker and that he should be happy at the thought.

He exclaimed into the dark, "Sorry! Not happy about it at all!"

Nor did he want the bomb to kill anyone else or have anyone become lost in searching for him. The thought caused a rise of guilt the equal of his fear; his life wasn't worth more than theirs.

Peter breathed deeply and shed a few more tears. He knew his father's dilemma: is it best to die if that avoids taking out anyone else? Peter didn't yet feel he could forgive his father; he was just becoming aware how forgiveness might be possible.

Peter felt for the slope, stood up, and walked downwards. He thought a mile should be about right. Captain Banbury's crew had measured out that much.

Of course, in the pitch black, it was difficult to judge speed or distance. He walked on, maybe a mile, maybe far more.

He sighed and swallowed. Kneeling on the hard rock, he quietly said an Our Father, a Hail Mary, and a Glory Be, and then let go of the button.

CHAPTER TWENTY

Sunday morning

In the early hours of Sunday morning, in the kitchen of the rectory at St. John's In The Green, Fred had put his helmet in the sink, for want of a better place. Fiona sat at the table engrossed in a call.

"Yes, sir...That's correct...Correct...No, not at this time...Yes, sir... Thank you. Yes...you too."

She put down her phone.

"What did he say?" asked Fred.

"Being a politician, he said nothing."

"Oh, you're not fired then?"

Fiona smiled and swore.

He sat opposite her. "What do we do?"

She thought for a while and said quietly, "I'm open to suggestions."

"There wasn't anything useful on the tapes at all?"

She shook her head. "Not that I could see. It's too blurred, too fast to make out what happened."

"But we thought we saw the bombers coming out the Manchester end...I mean in the afternoon?"

She nodded. "We let them go into the church here. We saw them... or someone very like them...come out up north, thinking it was their final reconnaissance. Maybe they were decoys. I'm starting to suspect the device may have been hidden in Wallace's tubs some time ago. The gang appeared out of this end as the fireworks began."

"And nothing to be seen later...with Peter?"

She shook her head. "Just as the civilians said. The three dragging the family didn't reappear at the other end. They must have been surprised at the resistance a girl, a couple of old folk, and a Morris dancer could muster! The only ones to come out...we have."

They were silent, replaying the movements in their minds.

"Get Wallace in," Fred said, "He might have some tricks. He might see more of Peter."

She nodded, "On his way."

"I'm willing to go through; you know that."

"He's not sitting on the path up against the wall." She sighed. "This...Reggie Smith...anything in what he said to help us?"

Fred paused and thought. "I thought he was a nutter. So...sorry, I wasn't hanging on every word."

"But I'm right in saying the boy only thought he'd been in there a short while."

"Oh, yeah...overnight at most."

"But decades passed."

Fred waited; he knew the look in her eye.

She stood up and moved his helmet aside to pour herself a glass of water. "So, in fifty years, Peter might walk out of there with a live bomb, and it might still go off."

"We'll have retired."

"I'll have you disappeared before you get a penny of your pension."

Fred chuckled and said, "Thanks!"

"Doing my bit for the national debt."

She sat down again, again sighing. "So, what is he? Unexploded ordnance? If he turns up, we deal with him just like kids who find hand grenades and lobstermen who haul up rusting hundred-pounders?"

Fred shrugged. "The longer it goes on...yeah. It's still possible it might go off tonight...I mean, this morning."

Fiona was silent for a while. "Read me his message again."

Fred took out his phone. "'Worked it out. Reggie is the key. He was #2 and okay. #1 wasn't' What the bloody hell is he on about?"

"I suspect there was supposed to be something else. People should make their points first, then chat."

"Probably should. But at least this means he was alive for a while in there. And wasn't under coercion when he sent this."

"And that he had some of his wits about him. Just not enough to say anything useful."

A loud knocking came from the front door.

Fiona frowned as Fred got up and went to the door.

Once inside, Hami shouted, "Is she 'ere?"

"Hold on, mate!"

Fred wasn't quick enough. Hami stormed into the kitchen.

"What the fuck have you done?"

"Excuse me?" said Fiona politely.

Hami pointed a finger close to her face. "You did nothing to protect our property! You let a riot happen, and you did nothing!"

"Sit down, Hami."

"I want answers!"

"Sit down, sir," said Fred pushing his chest against Hami's shoulder.

Hami flinched at the threat and sat down. Fred stood with his arms folded behind Hami's chair.

"You heard about the disorder, then," Fiona said.

Hami nodded, regaining his composure. "I also hear someone put a bomb in my mosque."

"Really? Who told you that?"

Hami shook his head. "Don't play games. Bomb? Yes or no?"

Fiona glanced at Fred.

She said, carefully, "Bomb. Neither yes nor no."

"Come on...What the fuck's that mean?"

"What was it you said to Peter about a great deed belittled by intention?"

Hami grinned. "It shut him up."

"And you had no more idea what it meant than I did."

"You're not shutting me up."

"It's in The Ambulatory."

"Oh, for fuck's sake!"

Fred leaned over Hami and said, "Is that how you preach to your congregation?"

"Yeah, it sounds even better in Arabic. So...what? It's in there, and what?"

Fiona shook her head. "Your guess is as good as mine."

Hami's eyes widened. "No...no, no, no. You know more than that. You always know. You've always got a plan. I want to know what you're..."

Fiona shrugged.

Hami held his head. " You're joking! You can't just leave it! It's right under...Come on!"

"I understand it could be anywhere between here and Manchester."

"You...You and that freaky tunnel!"

Hami was lost in thought. He looked at her, glanced over his shoulder, and suddenly stood up, backing his chair into Fred.

Without a word he moved toward the front door.

Fiona said loudly, "Everything we just discussed is classified."

Hami turned and stood in the kitchen doorway, his face like thunder.

Fiona continued, without looking at him. "And remember, there has been no sign-off as yet on your final development activities. I'm sure you wouldn't want to do anything to jeopardize your project."

Hami gagged slightly as if he were about to cry. "You mean, I wouldn't want to put a bomb under it."

Fiona smiled at him. "I'm glad we understand each other."

Hami punched the wall on his way out.

After the front door had slammed, Fred laughed and said, "Don't like him much, do you?"

"Oh, I'd much rather deal with him than Mufurrah-what's-it. Give me a worshiper of Mammon any day over a believer in God!"

"Yeah..." Fred thought for a moment. "Simpler, isn't it?"

"But we'll be dealing with someone else within the week."

"What makes you say that?"

"Hami's investment is suddenly subject to a risk he hadn't factored in. He won't live with the uncertainty; he'll pull out and find another toy to play with. The thought of protests or riots, lawsuits over land use and property boundaries—those he could twist for publicity. Now he thinks the whole thing could actually be destroyed. No...no profit, no glory."

* * *

Once it was light, Fred authorized the Morris dancers to leave the hall if they wished, the immediate emergency being over.

Several tidied away their bedrolls and yawning made their way through the park to the back of The White Hart in search of breakfast, news, or, failing that, gossip.

The smell of smoke hung over the closed-off street. The rectory was dark, and the church side door locked.

Fred chatted with a couple of PCs at the corner by the pub. An unmarked car, blue light flashing on its roof pulled up next to them.

"Morning, Fred!" called the passenger.

"Hey, Charlie," Fred replied, "What brings you out so early?"

"Heard you were having fun last night. Thought we'd check it out."

"All over, mate! You missed the party."

"Too bad. Listen, are you still on that machete murder?"

Fred shrugged, "Taken a back seat with all this. What've you got?"

"A body by the river, armed with something similar. Want a look?"

Fred nodded to the PCs and got into the back of the car.

* * *

The body was half in the mud exposed by low tide. He had been a muscular man, but now the water had begun to make him grotesque.

"Stuck here a couple of days at least," said Charlie, "Don't know if he fell or was pushed, but most like he went for a swim and hit his head on something in the water."

"What is he wearing?" Even as he asked, Fred knew. "Oh, shit!"

"Fancy dress."

Fred shook his head and said to himself, "Reggie is the key. He was okay. But the one who came out before wasn't okay."

Charlie frowned and said, "What did you say? Leather skirt, a shirt of leather straps? What's not fancy dress about it?"

"Cloak?"

"Didn't see one."

"Sandals?"

He looked down and shrugged. "Might have."

Fred swallowed and asked, "Sword?"

"Already bagged for you. I'll say that didn't come from a party shop. It's clean, sharp, and heavy. Brand new, by the look of it. A serious replica weapon. That's what made me think of you."

"Appreciate it."

"So you reckon this is your murderer? Or maybe your marauding transvestite?"

Fred shook his head. "Could be...That's the image people have, isn't it? Burly guy in a dress? Whereas your average trannie...you'd never really know. But, think about it. Someone like this comes at you with a weapon, such a surprise. So out of context, you kind of project your own interpretation on it, don't you?"

"What?"

"Nothing. Get the Path lab to call me when they're done."

"Will do."

"Oh, and, Charlie? This one's classified, okay? No idle gossip, no informal press.

"Really?"

Fred held up his finger in warning. "Spread the word. This one's mine."

Charlie shrugged his shoulders.

CHAPTER TWENTY-ONE

Friday afternoon

The Tea Rooms were a relic of the past. Hidden between newer buildings that permanently darkened the streets, the modest two stories went largely unnoticed by Londoners busy about their days—an advantage for those who wished to take tea privately.

Fiona had reserved one of the dark-paneled upper rooms for her meeting. The Reverend John Marx was last to arrive.

"Sorry to delay you all, there were leaves on the tracks at Crewe."

Fiona smiled and said, "We appreciate you taking the time to come by the conventional route. Please take a seat. You know Detective Mason and Bishop Davidson. This is James Welby, from the Home Office."

"How do you do?"

"Reverend."

Welby was a thin man, with short black hair that faded to silver in a singular streak along his left temple. He wore the anonymous dark suit of a career civil servant, and, were it still the fashion, perhaps would have worn a bowler hat.

John said, "I must confess I am puzzled to be summoned to such a meeting as this, and at the taxpayers' expense."

"Please help yourself to tea," said Fiona, "They are bringing more sandwiches. Don't be shy."

Dave muttered, "Not usually John's problem."

John smiled and said, "'Do all things heartily, as unto the Lord.' That's my motto."

Fiona began the meeting. "We have a problem."

The four men waited for her to continue.

She sighed and said, "It's called The Ambulatory."

John looked to Dave who smiled.

Dave said, "It's not a new problem. Each generation who lives next to it comes to this point eventually."

Fiona replied, "True. We might wish it were not so. But here we are, and there it is. It's been useful for a few, and an irritant for some. Its origins are as mysterious as they ever were. We may know less about it than did our ancient ancestors."

Fred said, "And now we have people coming out of it...you know... people from the past."

John frowned. "People? More than one?"

Fiona said, "Go on, Inspector."

"A body turned up in the Thames last Saturday afternoon, just before the riot: male, four foot nine, heavyset, dressed in...well, like a Roman soldier."

No one spoke.

He went on, "No ID. Unusual stomach contents. And...a sword. Best we can determine, it's the one that killed Fr. Samuels."

Dave asked, "And you think he came out of The Ambulatory?"

"Before I saw Reggie Smith, of course, I'd've said it was impossible. It's Peter Trowbridge's fault. He somehow knew Reggie was the real thing...really from 1940. I did not want to believe it. But his clothes, his gear, his vocabulary—the things he'd never seen. The nuns didn't want to believe it either. They tell me they do now. So, if you accept one person coming back...," he paused.

"Peter sent me a text message–we're guessing sometime just after he was pushed into the expanse–saying Reggie was the key and that Reggie was 'okay.' I had no idea what he meant and just assumed it was the start of a message Peter never finished. But, I think he meant 'what if someone came out of the past who wasn't okay? Someone with an attitude, or a mission, or someone who was a real nutter. Reggie was okay, in that he was harmless. As soon as I saw the Roman's body, how he was dressed...and that sword was exactly what we were looking for." Fred shrugged. "I think he came out of The Ambulatory and found his way up to the church and through to the rectory. What passed between him and Fr. Samuels I can't guess, but we know the result."

John muttered, "Extraordinary!"

Fred added, "It may be the Roman was scared out of his wits. And he would have given Fr. Samuels a hell of a fright."

Dave gasped and rolled his eyes. "Oh, poor Bart! He was probably one of the few people in the area who could have talked with a Roman. If they could have sat down and talked...Bart was a Latin scholar! It might not have been straightforward, but they could have communicated. What a tragic mischance!"

John coughed and said, "That events went so awry, Dave, could be just as easily explained by them actually having such a conversation. It was Bart this soldier met, don't forget. A man with the ability to instantly offend whomsoever he encountered, and probably, alas, not only in English."

Fiona involuntarily let her face slip into a smile.

Dave nodded, a sad smile on his face. "True, John, unfortunately true."

As they sat and digested this news, Fiona said quietly, "I hope you appreciate the present danger that we are now beginning to understand. One man with a sword caused one death and several injuries. What other bloody eras from England's past are going to throw killers out onto our streets? And...things less controllable. Black Death anyone? Some ancient invalid with a version of disease we no longer have perhaps? A lot of people have come and gone through that tunnel over a great many centuries. I'd say we were lucky with this one, doubly lucky with Reggie Smith. We cannot count on luck to save us a third time, nor onward into the future."

Dave shook his head. "This is troubling. But are you really thinking this thing is a public health risk?"

Fred said, "Both public health and public safety. If this bloke had had an army with him, they could have hacked their way halfway across town before we knew what was happening."

James Welby nodded but said nothing.

John shook his head. "But surely no one's ever seen this before. We've never heard of this happening. I've read a lot in the archives—some of it goes back a long, long way. I've never seen as much as a hint that anyone who got lost came out...later."

Fred said, "But people do get lost."

"Oh, yes, some quite famous cases...fights along the path and combatants disappearing into that darkness. Troubled children running in and not emerging the other side. Captain Banbury's crewman. That is, after all, why we have the warning signs."

Dave asked, "So what's happened? What was it about this Roman and young Reggie Smith?"

"Who—or what—is next?" asked Fiona before sipping her tea.

"Let's hope it's Peter," said John. He noticed Fiona's cup and saucer tremble slightly.

"Right!" Dave became more animated, "If we knew how it was done, what caused them to return, we might be able to get him out of there!"

Fiona shook her head.

Dave said to Fred, "You're the detective. Find out what the link between them is!"

Fred raised his hands. "I don't have a lot to go on, do I?"

In the silence that followed, Fiona said again, "As I said, we were lucky this time. How can we, in all good conscience leave The Ambulatory open, knowing what we now know?"

"But we don't know," said Dave, "That's what I just said. We have a chance to learn more. And at least one very good reason to: Peter."

John sat back in his chair and said, "I see now why we are here, Ms. Chapman. And why we are graced with the so-far-silent presence of Mr. Welby. Until the new man arrives In the Green, Dave and I are the ones who will have to implement any permanent closure you might order." He paused. "You want to know if we'll do it quietly."

Dave frowned. "What?"

John nodded. "You do have the power so to order, am I right?"

Fiona nodded. "If necessary. And I think it is. The only question is when."

Welby finally spoke. "It would seem that an immediate and permanent closure is the safest option."

Dave raised his hand. "Wait a minute!" He thought quickly. "Let's talk about the advantages of keeping it open."

Fiona shook her head. "What advantages?"

At that moment, the waitress arrived with two three-tiered plates of small sandwiches and then quickly departed the silent table.

"You were saying?" said Fiona.

Dave glanced at John hoping for help, then drained his teacup, and said, "Peter. We owe him every attempt at rescue."

"But...," Fiona began.

"I'm not done!" Dave's face reddened.

Surprised, she stopped and took a sandwich.

"Firstly, Peter! We have an absolute obligation to him. He put himself in harm's way for our benefit. Secondly, who else is in there? Who are we to seal them in? If there is a chance they can come out again, it's unconscionable not to attempt it. Thirdly, I would think the scientific community, let alone the historians, would lynch us all if they knew we even contemplated denying them access to the place... and to people...from the past. What these people could teach us!"

Fiona nodded. "What you say has weight. Peter...yes. But if we knew of any way to get him out, we would, of course, have done it by now. He may not have survived. Let's be realistic; it's unlikely he did."

Welby said, "As for the broader ethical argument, we have to balance the good we might do for any unknown persons trapped in the tunnel with the harm that might be done to our citizens, who, far from being unknown, are directly in our care."

John shook his head. "It's a lost cause, Dave. These good people will happily debate us till the cows come home. But the decision is already made."

Dave scowled at Fiona and poured more tea.

Fred who had sat quietly listening said, "No...I think you're wrong there, Reverend. And, though he's not here with us, I think Peter would say the same thing. Ms. Chapman said the question is when. Perhaps we should consider temporary measures? What are the possibilities before a closure happens? We could watch the entrances for any sign of more weird stuff. In fact, we should. I for one don't want anyone else taking explosives in there while we're watching the wrong bloody end and making us look like a bunch of amateurs! We could secure it without closing it up."

It was Fiona's turn to scowl.

Dave said, "Keep Wallace and his team on the job."

Fiona glanced at Welby. "He's privately funded. It's an issue."

Dave leaned across the table, his voice low but getting louder. "Not to you, it isn't. If you decide it's necessary, no one will say boo to you."

John smiled. "I have a suggestion."

Fiona turned deliberately away from Dave and toward John. "What suggestion?"

"Runners."

The others all frowned.

"Runners. Escorts, if you will. No one goes through without a guide. Everyone is checked and logged. You could even install metal detectors and turnstiles, if you like. That would address the risks of others going missing and anything nefarious being done."

Welby snorted and said, "The costs, man! The costs!"

John continued, "Declare it a site of special scientific interest, a historical monument, a part of the nation's travel infrastructure. Get the Lottery to chip in. You are the ones who fund all sorts of things about which the public never hears. Dave is right. Funding isn't an issue here, merely the will to do it!"

Dave nodded and said, "Runners? You know, you could have runners drawn from community service. In fact, I could use it as a discipline if someone steps out of line. I like that idea!"

"Let's not get carried away here," said Fiona.

Fred asked, "How long would it take to close it permanently? How would you do it?"

John and Dave thought. Dave said, "I wouldn't know how. Both ends would have to be sealed at the same time. I suppose you could get plasterers in and brick it up. I don't know if it would work."

John said, "I don't think it would. People have tried in years past. I've seen accounts that seem to indicate walls built to close the tunnel mouth blew out. Other barriers moved mysteriously. It may not be straightforward at all."

Fred said, "There you go, then. Secure it, put in the runners, keep it open while you study how to seal it. In fact, you might as well get gates across the entrances strong enough to keep anyone...odd...from coming out on their own."

Fiona looked from face to face.

"A year. One year, no more. You pay for these...runners."

Dave said, "And you fund both Wallace's stuff and Mason's gates."

Reluctantly she said, "Agreed."

She glanced at Welby. "We must go. Feel free to stay and have more tea. The Victoria Sponge is delightful. Thank you, gentlemen."

She stood and Welby followed.

In the silence after they had left, Dave chuckled to himself.

"Well, that," John said, "was interesting."

Dave said, "That will teach her to go head-to-head with two Doctors of Divinity."

John said to Fred, "Thank you for your help. What you did was very useful."

Fred shrugged. "They sent me on that damned mediation course. Had to come in handy sometime."

"So," said John, smiling, "More tea, please. How are we going to make the most of our year?"

CHAPTER TWENTY-TWO

Another month

The doorbell of the rectory at St. John's On the Green rang twice.
John Marx answered with his usual smile.

On his doorstep stood Ellie.

John lost his smile and asked, "How can I help you, Madam?"

"Reverend Marx, may I speak with you about access to The Ambulatory?"

"I'm sorry. You must refer all inquiries to the Working Committee in London. It's quite out of my hands at this point."

Ellie did not outwardly react. Instead she asked, "Then, perhaps, I might discuss some of the historical record with you. You told me once you keep a detailed archive."

"Mrs. Kingman, the archive is not open to the public."

She smiled. "I hardly count as a member of the public. The late Fr. Samuels spent much time telling me those same stories and sharing his theories with me."

John looked at his watch. "I'm sorry, I'm busy today. Perhaps you could write a formal request and I'll pass it on to the relevant authorities."

Ellie's eyes flashed at him. "Reverend Marx! You are the relevant authority. And I am asking you a second time for permission to review the archive!"

John smiled again. "Perhaps, Mrs. Kingman, you are unused to hearing the word "no," but in this case, I'm afraid I can only repeat myself. Good day."

The next morning, John awoke from a troubled sleep. He took longer than usual showering and eating breakfast. He stopped eating suddenly, at one point, fearing he had forgotten to open the doors for The Ambulatory's commuters. He sighed as he remembered and realized how much he missed them and that regular daily routine.

He stepped into his office, surveyed a scene of ruin and disarray, and called The Dave.

"Morning, Your Grace."

"Morning, heretic."

"I've been burgled."

"What?"

"Burgled. My files are all over the floor."

"Oh God! Did you see them?"

"Neither heard nor saw a thing. For all the mess, one would think the neighbors would have been calling in complaints."

"Call the police."

John sighed, "I suppose so."

"Can you tell if anything is missing? Any money gone?"

"Doesn't look like they even tried to open the safe."

"That's odd."

John sighed again and said, "No, not really. I turned away Bart's friend Ellie yesterday. She was after the archives again. I may have been a little short with her."

"She's a respected business woman, isn't she? She wouldn't stoop to something like that."

"No, of course. She'd hire someone."

"How much of it do you keep there?"

"Well, a lot. I've been studying in the light of...recent events. I'd had the museum ship a crate back. It's gone."

"See if the police can find any fingerprints."

"Will do. But I don't hold out much hope. If it were Ellie, she would undoubtedly employ competent and expensive professionals."

"I'll keep my ears open for news of her this end."

"Appreciated. I'll let you know more later."

"Thanks, John. Tell me, did you call me or your own bishop first?"

"He continues his unfaltering stance, neither wanting to hear, see, nor smell anything of The Ambulatory until he has retired into his dotage."

"Well, we can both empathize with him."

"Amen to that. Let's talk after lunch."

CHAPTER TWENTY-THREE

Another Monday night

Rick Dunlop was late. He hadn't realized being a father meant never being on time—never having enough time. He didn't wait to change at the end of the dancing. He stuffed his handkerchiefs into his pockets and hooked his bells together over his shoulder. He went straight down to The Ambulatory.

Riya had said she wanted him back early. She always said that. And then she had sent five texts during the evening practice. He wondered if the others had been through the same thing when their children were small—the wife constantly curtailing the husband's time away from home.

He still felt sick every time he had to go through the circular room at St. John's In The Green. Even with all the changes—the staff, the new signs, the crazy metal cage like a sieve around the tunnel mouth, the turnstile—it was still the same room where he'd watched Harry die.

Rick nodded to the runner, who put down her book and followed Rick into The Ambulatory.

* * *

Peter lay flat on his back on the hard stone for a long time just breathing and massaging his thumb.

I should move, he thought.

Say a prayer of thanks first.

Thanks, God. Much appreciated.

He took a couple of deep breaths and thought back over the

whirlwind he'd been in at St. John's: the constant activity, interruptions, tea making, the Morris dancers, the parishioners, the bizarre world of Fiona and her organization, the responsibilities on Fred's shoulders. It was so peaceful in the silence and the dark. He felt glad to be alive.

Go up the slope was the thought that occurred to him. He wasn't sure if it was his own thought or a response to his prayer.

As he walked up slowly, perhaps retracing his steps, perhaps not, he felt for a way to remove the briefcase. All he found was lengths of tape with no ends, sticking to his clothes and trying to stick to his fingers. He tucked the switch under his arm and it stuck to the tape.

It was as difficult to keep track of going up the slope as it had been going down. It was not steep. The gradient was subtle, and in the darkness, even up and down became blurred. The added weight of the bomb put his balance off to an extent that surprised him.

As he walked, he thought again about how Reggie had done this and how long he might have to do the same.

Was it an hour, a week, a month? He walked up, he rested, he felt for the slope, he walked, he rested, he walked up.

Then came the bird song—high-pitched, both faint yet gloriously loud in its difference from the silence. A ringing pulse came from above him, up the slope.

Peter ran, shouting nonsense in the dark.

He suddenly felt something soft, and his shoulder slammed against a vertical wall.

Rick shouted, "What the hell?"

Peter, gasping, said, "Who's that?"

"Peter? For fuck's sake! Peter?"

"I think so," he replied.

"Shit, man, where have you been? Jesus..."

Peter felt Rick's hand on his shoulder, supporting him.

"That thing is still on you!"

"Rick?"

"Yeah!"

Rick's runner called over his shoulder and said, "What's happening? Who the hell is that?"

"Shut up!" Rick snapped back.

Peter asked, "Um...Can you get this off me?"

"Well...If I could see...Let's keep going. Get into the light." To the runner, he said, "We're going on! Quick, into the light!"

"Let's all be careful! Don't let go of the wall," the runner replied with a shake in her voice.

"You don't have to tell us!" Rick said.

* * *

The Reverend John Marx was grinning widely as he brought Peter a mug of tea. He sat down next to him with his back against The Ambulatory wall. The yellow light from a lantern showed the shadowy walls and the smooth floor. They sat far enough around the first bend not to be able to see the opening.

"Bomb squad are on their way, Peter."

"Thanks."

"It's so good to see you. We all assumed the worst. And you've single handedly caused and removed the only blemish on my otherwise spotless record here."

Peter nodded. "Tea is good. Very good."

"And you, sir, are being very polite and not asking."

"I'm not sure I want to know. You're still alive, and so is Rick. I know I haven't done a Reggie Smith."

"No, far from it." John sighed. "Three years and a couple of months."

Peter nodded and continued sipping his tea.

"Are you in touch with Fiona?"

"Ah, the redoubtable Ms. Chapman. She will appear in due course, I'm sure. I think she got a promotion. But, of course, such things are not the currency of the common man."

"How about Reggie?"

John nodded. "Doing well. He misses you, I hear. Your uncle says he found a niche with the nuns. There is one whose memory has sadly regressed. He is a good companion for her apparently."

Peter laughed. "I'm lucky, so far. I could have turned up to find people zooming around with jetpacks and hover cars."

"Alas, sorry to disappoint. The government is still in charge, and the internet continues to suck the brains from our children."

"Good. Consistency. Very good."

"Ah, I hear the thud of military footwear. Your salvation, at least the physical side of it, has arrived."

Peter grabbed his arm. "Prayers welcome."

The vicar nodded. "Of course. Would you like me to stay?"

"No. You'd better not, just in case."

John, nodding, said, "All will be well, and all manner of things will be well," and went to meet the two officers from the bomb squad at the entrance.

They approached Peter slowly.

"Mr. Trowbridge?"

"That's me."

"I'm Major Hartnell; this is Sergeant Yardley."

"Thanks for coming. I really don't want you or anyone else getting hurt here."

"We know the risks, Mr. Trowbridge. No one forces us to do this. We're glad to be of assistance. Now, firstly, I, er...Ms. Chapman sends her regards and says to tell you you're late. If that makes any sense?"

Peter laughed, "Oh...no change there then."

Yardley set down two tripod-mounted lights. He switched them on and the tunnel flooded with white light.

"Now then, sir, what can you tell me about the device you're wearing?"

"The bomb has a dead man's switch that failed to trigger it."

"How long ago?"

Peter laughed a little louder than he should. "Remember where you are, Major."

As if on cue, the lights flickered, faded, and came back.

Major Hartnell glanced around. "Fair enough. Have you felt anything moving inside the case? Any ticking or clicking?"

"One click, maybe thud, when...when they did something with a cell phone, perhaps? After that, no. Oh, I did take a tumble. It would have been knocked about a bit then."

"Right. I think we'll try and get you out of it; then we'll go in and see what we've got. Yardley?"

"Sir."

Sergeant Yardley squatted next to Peter and said, "Lean forward, please, sir."

Peter tried to keep as still as possible as the tape and his sweatshirt fell to Yardley's knife.

Yardley said, "Easy does it!" and Peter felt himself free of the suitcase. "Slide to your right, please, sir."

Peter slid, and the two men held the briefcase in place as he moved away from it.

Without moving, Hartnell said, "Please join the reverend gentleman beyond the entrance, sir."

"Righto...good luck."

"Thank you, sir. Quick as you can!"

Peter felt guilty leaving them.

* * *

John and Peter sat together on the first step of the staircase, waiting.

After asking a few questions about the new cage surrounding the entrance, Peter lapsed into silence.

The soldiers' soft whispering came occasionally on the musty breath of The Ambulatory. Then the sound of Hartnell's boots again preceded him.

"Another prayer answered!" said the vicar.

Peter sighed.

"Thank you for waiting, gentlemen. All is well," said the Major.

"Was it faulty?" Peter asked.

"Not as far as we could see. It was ready to go off. Something in the electronics perhaps."

"But it's safe now?" asked John.

Hartnell nodded and said, "I'm going back in and we'll clear away the materials."

Hartnell, turned, picked up two additional lights, and went back into the mouth of The Ambulatory.

In the more relaxed silence that followed, John asked, "Hungry?"

"Not really. I could eat, I suppose, but I had a meal at the Morris Feast not long ago..."

"Ah, yes. You missed a good riot."

"I saw the opening shots, I believe."

"Several injuries. Only the one death...at the other entrance."

"Um...Did Harry have a family?"

"I believe so. But again, wherever Ms. Chapman goes, information becomes thin and chimerical."

"Is the mosque finished?"

"Ah...I think you'll find less of it than before. I understand the former owner is in court in an effort to extract his money and, in the grinding way such things are resolved, may be so for some years. I sense that the centuries of similarity between the churches is reestablishing itself."

"You know, I...I'm not sure what I do now..."

"You go home and see your mother."

"Oh God, she'll have thought I was dead!"

"We all thought that."

Peter was silent for a moment. "We don't have any traditional ways of dealing with resurrection do we...?"

"Oh, I suppose you're right," the vicar chuckled. "When one reads how Lazarus 'came forth' from his tomb, it's a bit underwhelming that Our Lord only says 'untie him and let him go'! One finds oneself thinking a little more fanfare might have been in order."

Peter laughed. "Perhaps my uncle can hire some mariachi."

"That's more like it! As soon as the way is clear once more, we'll go through."

Peter sighed and shook his head. "There's another thing...with Mother."

"Hmm?"

"Um...Um...I let go of the button."

"And?"

"No...I deliberately chose to let go. I walked out as far as I could. I wanted to avoid anyone else getting hurt."

John nodded. "Understood. A difficult choice in difficult circumstances."

"Did you know my father killed himself?"

John froze, his affable smile gone. "Oh dear...I see. I do remember Dave talking about..."

"I will have to tell her. I don't know how she'll take it."

"She'll be delighted to have you back."

Peter shook his head. "She's never forgiven him. Nor had I...but I think I...I understand something now I didn't before."

"Am I right that he left nothing by way of note or explanation?"

"No." Peter sighed. "It's The Great Family Mystery." He was silent for a long while. "I didn't want anyone else to get hurt. I thought about men like Fred, Hartnell, and Yardley—risking everything—I walked out a long way, hoping to ensure no collateral damage. I think...I wondered if Dad thought of himself as carrying a figurative bomb...as if he were a danger to us."

"Oh, Peter, how desperately sad," John said quietly.

"I, at least, had the excuse of an actual explosive device."

John nodded. "Please make sure you talk it over with Dave. He's family, and naturally knows more than I. But we can talk more. Use me as a second opinion if you will, if you need one. Now...I think you acted for the best, with the best intentions. I don't think anyone, least of all your own mother, would find fault in that."

They sat in silence for a long while.

"Can I take a train back?"

"Braveheart! I'll be with you all the way. No one ever goes in alone nowadays. That's what comes of three years of negotiating with the bureaucrats of Ms. Chapman's department. We've improved our procedures, you might say."

Just before they reentered the tunnel, John's phone beeped.

"Oh, it's for you. From Fred Mason. 'Number 3. Are you okay?' He has okay between asterisks."

Peter chuckled and said, "Tell him I'm sane and unarmed."

As John typed the message, he flashed Peter a mischievous grin. "Really?"

Peter smiled back. "Close enough."

* * *

Peter wasn't prepared for a week of celebrations, meals, and parties. When things calmed down, he felt tired and overfed. Standing in his mother's kitchen, drying dishes as his uncle washed them, he said, "I need another retreat."

"You've been alone for three years!"

"No, I haven't. I don't know how long it was, but it wasn't anything like that long for me."

"Right, right! It's difficult to...you know..."

Peter nodded. "I know. There is something I want to mention."

"Surely. What is it?"

"I might know how to get people out."

Dave stopped, water dripping from his hands.

Peter continued. "It's just a theory—no, a hypothesis, to be exact."

"Do you want to talk to Fiona about it, or is this something for John Marx and my new chap?"

"I suppose it'll have to be sanctioned officially. I...just don't want to do it, though."

"Peter?"

"With Reggie, it wasn't too long. We still speak his language. With the Roman? Look what happened! We have to be ready to deal with whoever we get. There's no way of knowing...Well, we need to be prepared, anyway. I don't want to do it at all, if we aren't really ready."

"I see what you mean. But as you saw, they've had us tighten it all up to prevent anyone getting out—unexpectedly. And no one new has been lost."

"I know. But no one else has come out, have they?"

"Only you."

Peter nodded. "Let's make a plan. Social services, paramedics, armed police, and at least one Morris dancer."

Dave laughed. "What? Ah, I see. You want to recreate the exact conditions. I must say it is going to sound a little odd. I'll get Fred to ask Ms. C., and see what she can do."

Peter stopped for a moment, pulled a letter out of his pocket, and handed it to his uncle. "Oh, and I got this today."

Mrs. P. Kingman
The Grange
Middle Uffet
Gloucestershire.
29 September 2013

My Dearest Peter,

I cannot tell you how delighted I am to have discovered that you are safe and well and have returned to us. What stories you must have to tell! I am building the most complete database of accounts of The Ambulatory, and I look forward to adding yours.

Since we last chatted there have been such unwelcome changes at the St. Johns. In addition, both my "boys" have moved on. Brad was poached by America, and Dr. Wallace had to acquiesce to some unfortunate promotion.
But, now you are back, I do hope I may call on you soon. I promise to bring custard tarts!

I am anxious to resume my researches on-site and yet hope to recruit you to my team. You have a fine mind, and I know you would be a great asset to us.

Please write back with a day when I may come down to visit.
All the very best to you and your mother.

Yours,

Ellie

Dave read the letter in silence. "She has a nerve, doesn't she?"

"I suspect she hopes to influence your decisions about The Ambulatory through me."

"Undoubtedly."

"She's clever. Though John Marx thinks she's mad."

"One can be both, Peter. Perhaps you should meet her."

Peter shook his head. "I don't know. She will probably be all over us if my scheme produces results."

His uncle gave him a conspiratorial look. "Not if Fiona deems it all classified. No one will ever know."

"Fair enough!"

* * *

The rebuilt Tandoori Palace was full. At the table were Fred and his wife Rose, Dave and John, Rick and Riya, and Fr. Bill Freeman, the new pastor of St. John's In The Green. He was a surprise to Peter. A tall man, with a little too much weight around his middle, but also a pair of sharp eyes that Peter was sure missed nothing.

Peter was relaxed, outwardly.

Fr. Bill mentioned how busy the rectory was day in, day out, compared to his previous parish.

Peter asked, "Does Ellie still visit?"

Fr. Bill looked puzzled. John Marx leant in to say, "Ellie has rarely been seen since the cages went up."

Peter thought for a moment. "Not what I expected. I thought she would have been there supervising."

To John, Bill asked, "Who is she?"

"A funder of scientific investigation into our very own Wonder of the World. Another moth drawn to its flame."

Peter added, "And keen on recruiting me to her team. She even offered me a job—of some sort."

Bill smiled and said, "Was the offer a good one?"

Peter shook his head, "All I remember was the promise of custard tarts."

John laughed and said, "Oh, I feel for you! Such temptation!" To Bill he said, "She is suspected in, but of course far beyond being actually accused of, a series of burglaries related to both items from the museum's collection and my own archives."

Bill replied, "Oh, I remember you lamenting lost material. She sounds a challenge. Let's see who gets to save her soul, shall we?"

The vicar and the priest smiled and shook hands.

During the meal, Peter asked Fr. Bill, "Do you believe in aliens, Bill?"

The priest coughed, "Well...what do you mean exactly?"

"I mean, short fellows with large black eyes, visiting Earth from some other habitable planet."

Bill looked at Peter to gauge if he was joking or not. "Actually, no. I've seen accounts of UFOs and abduction stories, hard to avoid nowadays. But, no, I haven't seen anything that would make me take the possibility seriously."

"Is it heretical to think they exist?"

"Oh no! I wouldn't think so. It's just a matter of whether they do or not. Either the Earth goes round the sun or it doesn't. It's just the evidence that's needed."

Peter nodded and ripped off a piece of naan bread. "Would we have to convert them, if we met them?"

Bill laughed and said, "That's a good question! But, I did read C. S. Lewis's trilogy a long time ago. We might not need to; they might be closer to God than we are!"

"I like that phrase about Jesus having 'other flocks' to attend to."

Bill frowned and shook his head. "Well, that's usually understood to be the gentile nations."

"But it's a nice thought that God's plan is bigger than just the Earth. I mean, with a universe this big, it would be such a waste."

Fr. Bill lifted his glass and touched Peter's with it. "Indeed!"

Peter said to Fred at the end of the meal, "So she isn't coming?"

Fred shook his head. "She wasn't sure. Her work makes it difficult... you know..."

Peter stood, leaned on his fists, and announced to the table, "Ladies and Gentlemen, are we ready?"

Amid general consent, they left the restaurant and made their way across the street, into the church and down to The Ambulatory.

Peter did not question Fred about ambulances, police tactics, or the provision of other services, but he noted with satisfaction the unmarked vans filling the small street outside the rectory.

In the round room, there was little conversation. Two armed policemen sat off to the left of the cage.

Peter asked Rick, "You have them?"

"Here you go!"

He handed Peter two sets of Morris bells. In response to Peter's frown, he took them back, turned Peter around and held them one by one to Peter's calves, buckling them at the back.

"All set!"

Peter nodded, gave a test jingle of each leg, and said, "Right...see you in a few minutes...perhaps."

The policemen stood. One followed Peter, and they squeezed through the turnstile and disappeared into the dank darkness.

The others all waited. No one spoke except Rose, who said, "This place gives me the creeps."

The jingling of bells came back as slowly as it had faded.

First came the policeman shaking his head and smiling.

Peter followed, holding the hand of a young girl, who was, perhaps, nine years old. Her dress was heavy cotton, with lace at the top and splatters of mud on the hem. Her hair was braided and tied with ribbon.

Her smiled warmed the room.

Peter said, "Hello, everyone. This is Jenny. She's been lost for a while; just like I was."

Rose stepped forward to greet her as she stepped out from the cage. "Oh hello, Jenny, love. My name's Rose..."

CHAPTER TWENTY-FOUR

Another weekday evening

Peter sat one evening with his uncle at a wooden table in a pub garden. The smell of damp grass mixed with drifting cigar smoke from another table.

He asked, "When you first asked me to go to St. John's, you knew about Fiona...that whole terrorism thing."

Dave answered, "Yes, yes. But, of course, I wasn't at liberty to tell you about it. John and I had had several classified briefings about The Ambulatory and the mosque...and the threats. As you might imagine, I didn't include Bart in any of that sort of thing."

"But you let me just walk into the thick of it, of those people. What were you thinking?"

"Well, my first thought was you were a warm body when I didn't have one to spare. But then, Peter...jobs like that...Fiona's, and Fred's for that matter...it does things to people. It eats away at them. They suspect everyone, see the worst in the world. You? You don't. You have a much healthier attitude. And you are completely without guile."

"Really? And that's good?"

"In my book it is. And I thought it might help. If for no other reason but to have you, a real human being, standing next to them. An example of what they used to be...and of whom they serve to protect. I don't know, call me old-fashioned, but I think that sort of thing still counts."

"Huh!" Peter looked at his glass.

They sat and sipped their beers for a while in comfortable silence.

A slight breeze cooled the air around them.

Dave asked, "Any more nightmares about being taken by aliens?"

Peter shook his head. "And still no idea what that photograph of Bart's was about."

Dave shook his head. "I can't imagine, with him gone, there's any way of finding out."

"Well, next time I'm abducted, I'll ask them," Peter said with a smile.

They sat quietly again, until Dave suddenly said, "What is it about those damn bells, do you think?"

Peter shrugged. "No one knows where the dancing comes from. What chance of knowing where the bells originated? But—I'd guess—someone worked out the right size and number, and the combination of frequencies that would have an effect in The Ambulatory."

"Some shaman, you mean?"

Peter nodded. "Call him a Druid scientist."

Dave laughed.

Peter continued, "But look what happened to what he discovered! You hand down something important from one generation to the next and what do they do with it? How many years until they forget the context...misinterpret the message?"

"Oh, Peter..." said Dave smiling.

"What?"

"What a priest you'd have made..."

Peter smiled sadly at his uncle over the rim of his glass but said, "I'm beginning to think I might be onto something, though."

"With The Ambulatory?"

Peter nodded. "Maybe this is my calling?"

"What you want to do when you grow up?"

"While I'm waiting to."

Peter went inside to the bar for the next round. When he returned to the garden, Fiona Chapman was sitting at the table, chatting with Dave.

"Peter."

"Fiona! This is a surprise."

"Sorry I missed the dinner.

"You heard the result."

She nodded. "I came with a...suggestion. An offer, perhaps. But, I hear from your uncle, you are already on board."

Peter sat and glared at her. He downed half his beer in one go and said, "What offer?"

"We can turn The Ambulatory and...what you are doing...over to one of The Prince's Charities. That way we can assure you of funding and all necessary support, without unnecessary scrutiny or publicity."

"Assure who? Me?"

"We need someone discreet to run it. And you've already signed the Official Secrets Act."

Dave shook his head. "It's a funny business. And I–well, we all— worry it could be dangerous."

Peter shrugged. "It already was."

He and his uncle, both with grim smiles, raised their glasses together with a clink.

Peter asked, "Salary?"

Fiona answered, "Not a problem."

Peter shook his head and looked out over the pub garden. "It'll have to be a better offer than Ellie was going to make."

"Ellie Kingman?"

"Just sent me a letter saying she's keen to renew our acquaintance. After me for 'her team.'"

"You're not seriously considering it?"

"I was actually. While she seems to some to be a harmless old dear, John Marx thinks she is mad, and he might be right. It's fascinating. I'd love to try reconciling her manner, her obsession with The Ambulatory, with her running a biotech company." He shrugged. "And I hear she has acquired, by fair means or foul, a collection of materials associated with The Ambulatory unlike anyone else's. She told me I have a good mind. I thought I could usefully apply it to studying her."

"I would prefer we kept The Ambulatory within the family, so to speak. As I said, your salary–and its potential size–presents no problem. Are we agreed?"

She held out her hand and Peter shook it.

Fiona asked Dave, "Can you arrange for Peter to have an office and a room at the rectory?"

"Really?"

"We'll need an official address for the paperwork. Some continuity of presence will help keep up appearances for donors in the know."

Dave asked Peter, "Would you want to stay there?"

Peter shook his head. "No. But I suppose I would be out of Mum's hair. She's...still...finding the circumstances of my return difficult."

Dave nodded and said, "Give her time. It was tough on her."

Peter nodded.

Fiona said, "Well, we'll call that settled. I'll have the charity people formalize things. And, gentlemen, you can mark this day; I admit I was wrong."

Peter frowned. "About?"

"You. When we first met, I thought you were a bad idea. I gave Fred Mason hell over you. I was wrong."

"Can I get that in writing?" asked Dave.

"I'd make you eat it," she said smiling.

To both Dave and Peter's surprise, Fiona went to the bar to bring another round. She came back and handed Peter his wallet saying, "The barman says you left this on the bar last time."

Peter frowned, nodded and slipped his wallet back into his pocket. "Can't believe I did that..."

Long after Fiona left, Peter and Dave sat watching the twilight gather with few words passing between them.

Dave said, "Shame about Bart..."

"Terrible way to go," Peter agreed.

"Well...you know, I wonder about that. At least when he was 'done in,' he was 'done in' in Latin. You know, all in all, he would have appreciated that."

The *Ambulatory* Glossary of Unfamiliar Terms

alright? A variation on "How are you?"

As-salamu alaykum. The traditional Islamic greeting. Variations may apply depending on to whom the greeting is expressed and the orthodoxy of the greeter.

Bagman. In Morris dancing, the keeper of the bag, treasurer

boffin. A person engaged in scientific or technical research

fruit machines. One-armed bandits, slot machines; largely now all computerized

in the know. In on the secret

isn't it? A generic tag question, such as "aren't we?" and "don't you?" equivalent to the French "n'est-ce pas?" that via the British Asian community has come to be used in many cases where it may not be grammatical and often sounds counterintuitive

little oink. An annoying person with too high an opinion of himself; usually male

Morris dancing. An ancient folk tradition mainly found in the south of England, with variants in the north

Ragman. In Morris dancing, the overseer of costumery

several pints the better. Slightly inebriated

swot. A student who studies too much, perhaps to impress teachers

Ta. Thank you

torches. Flashlights

watch out. To be generally on guard

About the Author

Ed Charlton grew up in England. After many years toiling in corporate data systems, he followed his true calling: books and writing. Since 2005, Ed has supplied services to indie authors through his company Scribbulations LLC and writes constantly.

In 1963, Ed was part of the original target demographic for Doctor Who, long before society realized the effect of sci-fi on the young. As an adult, he has a reputation for asking, in the middle of long BBC dramas, "When do the aliens land?"

He is a member of the Science Fiction Association of Bergen County, NJ, and the founder of The Write Group: Kennett Square.

Ed writes science fiction in the classic mold—with humor and intelligence.

For other books by Ed Charlton, go to
edcharlton.com

The Problem with Uncle Teddy's Memoir
(Book One of the Aleronde Trilogy)

What exactly is *The Problem with Uncle Teddy's Memoir?*
And what is *A Speculative Fiction Romantic Adventure Mystery?*

Theo Kingman inherited a problem: great-uncle Teddy's unpublished memoir of an impossible life in the fabulous city called Aleronde. What are Theo's motives for selectively sending chapters to his childhood friend and publisher, Curt? Why does Curt find some of the descriptions so disturbingly familiar?

In copied letters, collected emails, office notes, and of course, the pages of Uncle Teddy's own manuscript, Ed Charlton pieces together a tale of empire, conquest, slavery, betrayal, romance, adventure, and mystery. Is it speculative? Is it even fiction at all...?

"The Problem with Uncle Teddy's Memoir is a tantalizing, disturbing little story, carefully and lovingly designed to maximize suspense and provoke thought."
                                                            - IndieReader. 4 Stars

Aleronde The Great

(Book Three of the Aleronde Trilogy, publication 2019).

The culmination of the events explored in both *The Problem with Uncle Teddy's Memoir* and *Saint John's Ambulatory.*

When a party from Earth find their way to the wonderful city of Aleronde, what will they find? Will the empire of Aleronde survive? Should it?

The ABLE Serial

Jim Able works in outer space. Although he has returned to duty after a disastrous encounter on a previous assignment, he is determined to enjoy his work. His boss may be on his case, but he still manages to drink a little too much, to eat dubious food, and to smell the alien flora.

The first episodes find Jim sent to Turcanis Major V to solve a mystery but with strict instructions not to start a war. Will he find the alien calling himself "Edward of Turcania"? Will he discover who has qualified for the First Contact reward? Will he accidentally foment a revolution?

"Thoroughly enjoyed reading this entertaining, intriguing and fast paced series. I was impressed that the author was able to touch on a number of themes - especially the "science vs. religion conflict" without interrupting the narrative. I appreciate how well the author was able to describe future technology with just enough detail to make the story plausible without distracting the reader.

This is a saga but done with a light touch. It's disarming and, before you realize it, you're hooked!"

- An Amazon reviewer

Made in the USA
Middletown, DE
20 September 2018